Praise for T

"A gripping and thoughtful read infused with the richness of Jewish culture."

—Dr. Celia Nyamweru, Professor (Emerita) Anthropology, St. Lawrence University

"A riveting, intimate tale, with far-reaching cultural consequence, *The Path to God's Promise* challenges the notion that prophecy is over. Through Elinor's personal struggle to face her doubts, heal her trauma, and own her profound relationship with God, this story sends an essential message for our time: only through our free will can we divert humanity from impending climate catastrophe."

—Rabbi Zelig Golden, Founder, Wilderness Torah

"Five mass extinctions in earth's history have been identified—all the result of natural events. A sixth may be imminent and unavoidable, this time triggered by human activity. This novel, written not from a scientific perspective, but from insights profoundly spiritual and cultural, presents both cataclysmic and hopeful alternatives; the choice is ours. A thoughtful and provocative read."

—Dr. Paul Robinson, Professor and Director (Emeritus) Human Needs and Global Resources, Wheaton College

"Ahuva Batya Scharff's, *The Path to God's Promise* is gripping in its honesty and intensity, yet also manages to be humble, personal, and playful in a way that drew me in and kept me turning the pages. Equal parts frightening and inspiring, this is a deeply informed, compassionate and, yes, visionary, Jewish response to our present moment of truth as we face both the imminent likelihood of planetary calamity and, simultaneously, a growing shift in consciousness toward a path of caring, connection, flourishing, and holiness."

—Rabbi Natan Margalit, PhD, Author, *The Pearl and the Flame: A Journey into Jewish Wisdom and Ecological Thinking*

Ahuva Batya Scharff

THE PATH TO GOD'S PROMISE

AUSTIN MACAULEY PUBLISHERS™

LONDON • CAMBRIDGE • NEW YORK • SHARJAH

A CIP catalogue record for this title is available from the British Library.

ISBN 9781035820986 (Paperback)
ISBN 9781035820993 (ePub e-book)

www.austinmacauley.com

First Published 2023
Austin Macauley Publishers Ltd®
1 Canada Square
Canary Wharf
London
E14 5AA

To Gen Z
You have the power to change the rules.

קום לך אל־נינוה העיר הגדולה וקרא עליה כי־עלתה רעתם לפני

Go at once to Ninevah, that great city, and
proclaim judgement upon it, for their wickedness has
come before Me.
Jonah 1:2

Chapter One

עורי עורי דבורה עורי עורי דברי־שיר

Awake! Awake, Devorah! Awake, awake and sing!
– Judges 5:12

Be careful what you wish for. As a child, I wished only to be near God. If I'd understood the consequences of wishing, of prayer, I probably would have wished for something else. I suppose I should start at the beginning.

My earliest memory is of God speaking to me. I was four. I climbed the thick-branched tree outside our old farmhouse in California's San Joaquin Valley to lie on one of the limbs. It was early summer. The light breeze made the hair on my arms stand up. I smiled at the way the sun came speckled through the canopy, dappling my skin. While I was delighting in the experience of sun and wind, I heard God's whispered voice. God said, "You belong to Me."

My mother, more superstitious than religious, named me for greatness: Elinor Shefa Simentov. It is the perfect name for a Jewish mystic. Simentov, our family name, means 'good signs' in Hebrew—as in signs and omens. Shefa, my middle name, is usually translated as 'abundance,' but it can also mean 'divine emanation' or 'flow.' In Arabic, it means

9

'recovery' or 'healing.' Elinor translates from Hebrew as 'God is my light.' You could say just from my name that I was fated for a single purpose. But prophecy is a difficult thing for a contemporary Jew. It is not a gift that is accepted in the 21st century, not in my community. And yet I can no longer deny who and what I am.

At first, my visions were simple and comforting. Throughout my childhood, I had a dream about a wall of flowers: blue, deep red, and purple. There was no action, no conversation, just a single picture of a wall covered in a cascade of dark green leaves, vines, and flowers. It cheered me. The vision recurred every year or two until I was nineteen. While on a semester abroad in India, I walked into our classroom at a facility in Pune, turned to my left, and saw through the sliding glass doors that familiar flowered wall. I was shocked. I stared at it for hours on end during our six weeks of classes at the site. Of course, after my stint in Pune, I never dreamed of that wall again. But at the time, seeing the wall encouraged me. It made me feel I was in the right place. More than déjà vu, this was an actual vision that I had recorded in the journals I kept in my youth. It was confirmation to me of my visionary capacity.

Other than a few single images like the one I had of the wall, the visions I have rarely have anything to do with me. I do not have the ability to see lottery numbers. When I try to apply my gift for personal reward, the outcomes are poor. When I know which horse is going to win the Kentucky Derby, I write the winner's name on a piece of paper—but the instant I put a wager on the animal, I lose. I am accurate when I have nothing to gain, when the visions are a touchstone, reassurance, or warning. I am not a fortune teller. I am a vessel through which visions come. I do not get to choose the channel on the TV.

I look at myself in the full-length mirror in my bedroom, contemplating who I am. The mirror is five feet tall in a dark frame and looks more expensive than it was. The room is shadowy. The only light on is on the bedside table far behind me. Though it is dark, I see myself clearly. I am a typical-looking, if heavy, Jewish woman. Three hundred pounds with all the weight in the middle—pendulous breasts and a protruding belly, no butt. I am an apple on thick legs. My stature is a little taller than the average woman, five feet seven, but I seem much taller, not only because of my weight; it's my presence. I can dominate a room without trying. I'm in a constant battle to 'pull it back'—a phrase I say to myself so often that it has almost become my mantra. My near-black hair is a tumble of curls that, instead of getting longer, gets tighter. The hair grows. I can tell because I have to dye the grey roots, but the length does not change. It stays just below my chin year after year. Everywhere I travel, especially in the Middle East, I am immediately recognized as a Jew. I look like my people.

In front of the mirror, I sigh. My hands caress the belly that hangs heavy under my cheap t-shirt. I think about losing weight. It might be possible if only I was willing to eat fewer latkes. And chimichangas. I sigh again. The effort to be thinner is daunting.

I lean closer to the mirror to examine my face. There are no lines on my skin or bags under my eyes. I do not look my forty-five years. I attribute my youthful appearance to not having had children. My peers who had children early, before twenty-five, have aged well, but my friends who had children

11

later, especially those who waited until their late thirties or forties, for the most part, have had the life-force sucked out of them. They look shriveled and old. Those who also have to work a full-time job in addition to raising their children have withered on the vine. I gaze at my reflection more closely. The fat helps, too. My facial features are plump and in place. Fat faces crease less than thin ones. Maybe latkes and chimichangas aren't so bad after all.

"Can I really be what God wants?" I ask myself silently as I leave my place in front of the mirror to flop down on my bed. Forty-five. Fat. Barren. Not in particularly good health. No boyfriend, husband, or prospects. A spinster. An also-ran who smiles at a bris and sobs later a block down the road, alone in a parked car, because I will never, ever be that beaming mother. Oh sure, I'm flourishing in my career, but that's the norm in my community. Successful is an adjective applied to almost every Jew I know who works. We're all a successful doctor, lawyer, professor, artist, scientist, teacher, inventor, nonprofit executive, or entrepreneur. In my community, accolades and awards are as ordinary as taxes. What I am though, is a failure in the way that most counts. I did not fulfil what some argue is the primary mitzvah. I was unable to have a child to carry on our traditions.

I think about God and the task set before me. As I lie with my eyes closed, I recall how two months earlier God approached me about doing something important and constructive with the visions I have.

I was in Pacific Palisades, a beach suburb on the Westside of Los Angeles. It's an affluent neighborhood with multimillion-dollar homes perched on the cliffs overlooking the Pacific Ocean. Pali, as it is sometimes called locally, is nestled between Santa Monica and Malibu. Having lived in Los Angeles for many years and gotten sober there, I often return to the area to celebrate important recovery anniversaries with my friends in Alcoholics Anonymous. This year, I reached twenty years clean and flew to Los Angeles to get my twenty-year medallion at a big Monday night meeting in Pali.

It wasn't my regular meeting, the home group I attended faithfully every week for more than ten years. That meeting, on a Friday, I could not make. Not only did I have a writing deadline that prevented me from traveling on Friday, but my sponsor, who has been my sponsor for all of my twenty years sober, now lives in the Palisades. With her three kids, the Pali meeting was more convenient for her than Brentwood, where we usually met when I lived in town.

After the speaker—a Hollywood A-lister more than forty years clean—had finished with his call to recovery, which led to a standing ovation, it was time for the 'birthdays.' I was allowed to speak for three minutes about being twenty years clean. My sponsor presented my cake. I thanked her and the A-list actor. Twenty years earlier, he had found a chair for me to sit on in a different crowded room. I was only a few days sober then and too sick to get to the meeting early enough to get a seat. I stood, desperately ill, sweating, and mildly suicidal, beside a garbage can. I was fairly certain that I was going to vomit. He saw me there, ordered someone to get me a chair, and helped hold me up while we waited for the seat to arrive. Then this very famous man looked me in the eye and told me that I was the most important person in the room. He asked me, as if he could read my mind, not to kill myself that day. He didn't remember his kindness to me, but I did and thanked him. He kissed me in front of everyone as I walked back to my seat.

Two friends, who had come to town for the event, took me out to celebrate at dinner after the meeting. We went to a busy Italian restaurant on the Promenade in Santa Monica. Izzy and Amanda were not alcoholics, but were extremely supportive of my recovery. Neither could believe that a famous movie star had kissed me in front of several hundred people. I laughed. It's the kind of thing that happens all the time in meetings, but I didn't tell them that. I let them enjoy the 'specialness' of the occasion. 'And shouldn't we do just that?' I thought to myself, 'Being sober for twenty years is special.'

"I can't believe it," Izzy said in her thick Australian accent as the waitress refilled my water glass. I could barely hear her over the bustle and loud conversation. "I remember when you hid beer in the cattle grate at that summer camp we worked at in Montana," she said. I smiled, recalling her look of utter revulsion when I pulled two cold beers from between the grate's metal bars and offered her one. "I knew then," Izzy continued to Amanda, her wife, "that we had a real problem. Anyone who hides beer like that—"

I interrupted. "I also used to keep whiskey in a shampoo bottle," I said, making sure that the salad on my fork had just the right chicken to vegetables ratio. "That's why I never let you borrow my stuff and I never, ever took a shower unless I was alone." I put the salad into my mouth as my friends looked at me, dumbfounded.

"I had no idea," Izzy said.

"I am a real alcoholic," I said. "And by some miracle, I have not had a drink in twenty years and three days."

My companions held up their water glasses. I did, too. "To twenty years of recovery from hopeless alcoholism and a kiss from you-know-who," Amanda said. We clinked our glasses and laughed.

That night I was alone in my room, a garage converted into a guest house that my cousin generously allows me to borrow when I visit. I like staying there. It is quiet with a bed so comfortable that it's hard to get going in the morning. If I crack the window over the door slightly, the scent of the garden, of the carefully tended roses, wafts in on the breeze that comes inland from the sea.

I sat on the bed in meditation and felt the familiar draw of God calling me. My breathing slowed in a practiced way as I opened my spirit to a consciousness beyond our everyday shared reality. As my breathing reduced to only a few breaths per minute, I loosed my soul from the bindings that keep it anchored in my body, allowing myself to be brought to the place where I most often meet God.

Our spot, as I affectionately think of it, is a fallen tree on a meadow's edge. The meadow is expansive and seems to be in a state of perpetual spring or early summer. There are wildflowers in the verdant, ankle-high grass. The log is enormous. It's almost too tall to sit on. The tree trunk is smooth and comfortable, the rough bark long ago stripped away by time and weather. Behind it is a forest, a mix of deciduous trees and evergreens. The scent of the place is intoxicating. It smells intensely of pine with hints of wildflowers.

When I sat down on the log, God was already waiting for me. "I want to talk with you about a project that I would like you to complete," God said.

In my visions, God has no form. God presents to me as a kind of heat shimmer that is roughly the size of a man. God has no shape or substance, only an intensity of being and ethereal beauty that are instantly recognizable to me as God. I realize that this appearance is an illusion. It is an access point. God creates it to give me something to hold onto, to communicate with because God's true manner and nature are incomprehensible. I hear a male voice that speaks English because that is what makes it easiest for us to be in relationship, not because God is male or human or English-speaking. God's true nature cannot be described in such terms. What I see is not who or what God is. It is a small piece of divinity that is knowable, but only 'true' to the extent that a pine needle is descriptive of the tree from which it falls.

I smile. Although I am in awe of God's power and presence, God is also my closest confidant and friend. This has been the case the whole of my life. As a young child, I would burst into tears whenever the *V'ahavta* was chanted: "You will love the Lord your God with all your heart, with all your soul, and with all your might." I cried because I did love God. I loved Him so much that the mere mention of that love brought tears, and I would throw myself on the synagogue's floor, proclaiming, "I love you, God! I love you!"

My childish fits embarrassed my parents, who would pull me from the floor and hurry out of the sanctuary with me still wailing about my love for God. The other congregants at the shul would smile and shake their heads. It wasn't often that children were removed from services for proclaiming their love for God, though admittedly I was quite loud about it.

While I may no longer have thrown myself on the floor at the shul, my love for God had not changed. I had been receiving visions all my life, and this was how I expressed what that felt like. At least, that's what I thought before God asked for my devotion to be expressed in action. I was no less sure of my love but far less certain that I could convey my commitment to God in the ways He wanted.

"I want you to be My emissary, My prophet. I would like you to speak truth to power and get a message out to as many people as you possibly can. This world needs to hear My voice in a vibrant and meaningful way," God said. God's presence comforted me. It felt as if He smiled as He spoke. For the most part, with me, God is affable and pleasant. Although I have never asked God about it, I am aware that God chooses this presentation for me, allows me to hear Him in a way that will soothe and calm me. God's is a strong voice, a voice that makes me feel safe.

"No."

God laughed, a deep and throaty sound. I imagined that if God ever took human form for me, He'd look like Dan Haggerty, the actor who played Grizzly Adams on TV in the 1970s, rugged, handsome, and a little bit wild. "That was a quick response."

"Since when does doing anything You ask lead to good for the one You ask it of?" Prophecy is painful for all prophets. I thought about the prophets in the Tanakh. Which of them ever had a good life by doing what God asked of them? Moses, the most revered of our prophets and leaders, had not gotten to enter the Promised Land and had had to put up with decades of people refusing to do what he requested. His experience was the norm for visionaries. People rarely listen to God's prophets, except Jonah, who was miserable anyway. It's a lifetime of headache for the seer. Didn't

17

Jeremiah, the unluckiest of the prophets, suffer directly not just from his visions, but from the first-hand experience of the Babylonians sacking Jerusalem and sending Israel into exile?

In tractate *Bava Batra* of the Talmud, the rabbis concluded that after the fall of the Second Temple, prophecy is given only to children and madmen. By this time, I was no longer young and at least in my own opinion, not at all mad. I wanted no part of whatever God wanted from me. I didn't desire to be a seer. If I had to be a visionary or prophet, we could stop at visions of flowered walls.

God said nothing for some time, waiting for me to explain myself. When I did not, He asked, "What is your concern?"

I did not immediately respond. My head flooded with dozens of reasons why I did not even want to hear God's request, let alone fulfil it. Finally, I settled on a specific reason, "I do not want You to show me events that I am powerless to change."

****

A year earlier, I sat in tears in the rabbi's office. A week before that we had both been in Jerusalem, he at an educational seminar, me visiting a friend. Rockets were launched from Gaza, dozens of them. Even in Jerusalem, we were not safe. The missile-alert sirens went off three times, shrilly screaming at us that we had seconds to flee for safety. During the third alarm, I watched the Iron Dome defense system hit one of the incoming rockets. I was leaving an art gallery near the King David Hotel, where I had purchased a painting by Kadishman. They had given me a 'get it out of the country' price that I could not pass up. The art dealer and I stood in this doorway, gaping as the Iron Dome took out the Palestinian projectile. We watched the debris fall into the garden at the YMCA.

While this violence was going on in Israel, I had a terrible recurring dream. Each morning for a week, in the moments before I awoke, I saw a plane being hit by a missile. I called the rabbi at the apartment he had sublet in Jerusalem. "A plane is going to be hit by a missile, but I don't know where or when. Soon. Soon," I babbled.

"You don't know that," he said, trying to calm me, a note of irritation in his voice. I must have interrupted him while he studied. He viewed his study time as sacred.

I wasn't to be put off. This was a desperate situation in which hundreds of people would be killed. "You're not hearing me!" I shouted. "It could be one of our planes. We leave here in the next two days."

"You'll be fine," he said. "We'll both be fine." He paused. "And if you don't know which plane will be hit, what can you do?"

He was right. What could I do? Call the FAA or the U. S. Embassy and say that I had a dream that a plane would be hit by a missile somewhere in the world at some point in the next few days? There are special places for people who bother the authorities with information like that. They're called asylums, and I didn't care to be admitted to one. Still, the dreams continued.

Three days later, a passenger plane was shot down over Ukraine. It was filled with research scientists on their way to Australia for a conference on HIV/AIDS. A cure for AIDS was probably percolating in the mind of one of those medical researchers, and in an instant, it was gone.

I thought about that experience of helplessness as I sat in the rabbi's office, where I had been ushered following evening minyan. At the end of Ma'ariv, during the *Kaddish Yasom*, I had run from the room to throw up in a little garbage can in the seminar room across the hall. I did not want to be an ineffective prophet, a seer who was unable to help those around her. But who listens to visionaries? Prophecy is an inefficient system of communication. Seers and mystics always have incomplete information. Visions are open to interpretation. In the present, a person who doesn't have visions might think, 'The vision means no one should shoot down planes,' and they are right. That is one meaning. But each soldier with his head full of politics and orders doesn't believe that he is the one God is speaking to. If he believes in God, God, in his view, is on his side.

What was clear to me was that my visions made me ill. They made me feel culpable and complicit, even though I was never given enough information to take action. As I cried over the deaths of those people on the airplane and complained through tears to the rabbi that it sickened me to receive visions about incidents I could not keep from coming to pass, he had one piece of advice. "If that's how you feel, then tell God."

God asked, "Why are you refusing the gift of prophecy?"

I snorted. "Prophecy is no gift." I paused, sitting silently for several minutes. "I will not be involved in futile attempts to intervene in a future I am powerless over."

"How do you know that you cannot influence others?" God asked. He seemed profoundly perplexed. "You are the messenger. You have no idea how another will act."

I was irritated. "You show me bits and pieces of events that have no timeline. I want to know what the deadline is for action and who is supposed to take that action. I want specifics. That's what's needed for people to believe. Specifics and context are the best ways to coax engagement."

"What if I told you that I cannot give a clearer picture because it takes away free will?"

"Then I'd say that You should show the visions directly to the people who are doing the bad things and not show me the awful aftermath of their choices."

God seemed to think about this for a moment. Then He said, "The visions received by prophets and mystics are meant to sway people to right action. Isn't the message of the prophets, 'If you do these things, this will be the terrible result; turn from your current path?' A prophet isn't a psychic who tells what will happen. I don't give the warning in order to prove that poor choices have horrible consequences, but to show that doing what I suggest is the best path for the community. The most effective prophets are the ones who are wrong in predicting the future because the people take a new course—like Jonah, to whom the people did listen. The message about the plane that you had while you were in Israel,"—I turned my head toward God, frowning—"was not that you could have changed that specific event. This was a message meant for you to believe in yourself and the authenticity of your prophetic gift."

I nodded slowly. That was not an answer I liked. "You didn't tell me who that vision was for," I said, "because that person's mind and course were already set. I wasn't ever meant to do anything."

God said nothing, allowing me to digest my comment. Sometimes prophets see visions of situations they cannot change, and that is simply part of the burden they bear. God was asking me to believe not only in Him, but in myself. God wanted my complete trust. It was a tough ask.

"I want you to write a book," God continued. His tone shifted to one of great seriousness. We were no longer talking about me and my insecurities. God had a request and was making it. "Prophecy is not so much about predicting single events, but making sea change. You are a writer, so a book will be your instrument. It is time to share a warning about the way humankind lives. Your relationship with the planet and one another is untenable. It cannot continue. If humankind carries on living as it does, with an ever-expanding need to consume, you all will all perish. This is something you, Elinor, can affect."

I thought about all the scientific evidence piling up regarding climate change. I had seen droughts ravage East Africa. As a student, I carried food to those in need on the border between Kenya and South Sudan. I had witnessed powerful hurricanes hit the USA's East and South. The intensity of wildfires had grown beyond comprehension. And the suffering of the animals. I couldn't help but think of the images of polar bears starving to death. It was unthinkable that those giant, majestic animals faced extinction. "But that's Your will, isn't it? Isn't climate change a punishment for our inappropriate actions?" I thought about the dominant culture around me, full of people who believe that God punishes us for making choices He doesn't like. Some people call these actions 'sin.' I wasn't sure what I believed.

"It most certainly is not, not in the way you are suggesting," God said, responding sharply to my accusation. "Whatever happens to humankind is your own doing. It has nothing to do with Me."

I looked in God's direction. "It has everything to do with You, at least that's how visions are interpreted. Prophecy is always written with the same message. The people have misbehaved and, as a result, You will punish us. Humans use the old prophets and prophecies as proof of God's will when cataclysm occurs. 'The hurricane hit New Orleans because the residents are sinners,' is an argument that some Christian fundamentalists have made. They call it Your punishment for sin. Instead of trying to prevent wars and pestilence, groups of many sorts foment these events as proof of Your disapproval of certain acts, suggesting from the works of the prophets that destruction is Your will."

"You think I want you to write a book about how I will punish humankind for their greed and gluttony?" God asked.

"What else would a prophet write about?" I asked. "Whether our demise is of our own making or not, isn't destruction the only outcome possible?" God did not immediately respond, so I continued. "I'm not just saying no to the book, God, I'm saying no to being Your spokesperson. I don't want to be Your envoy. I want my relationship with You to be private, not part of a public spectacle."

God remained silent. I watched the breeze move the grass in front of me. The weather was warm and comfortable. I waited.

God began to speak. I kept my eyes on the grass, though I listened carefully. "Humans on Earth are killing themselves and most life on the planet. Climate change is a real threat to humankind's survival. Humankind was not created to ravage the planet in an unending quest for riches, impoverishing the majority while a small number revel in incomprehensible wealth."

God paused. I looked in His direction and nodded. I was listening. He continued, "I am going to show you visions of the past and future. I want you to share them as you experience them, and write them down as a chronicler of events, like Dante's writing in *Inferno*. You are going to take a trip with Me, and you are going to tell the world."

"Not hardly," I said, half under my breath.

God ignored my remark. "You do not have any responsibility for the outcome. People will listen to the warning or they will not, and yours will be one of many voices calling out. There are scientists, artists, and seers from all parts of the globe, all religions, who will use their talents, in different ways, to share this message. You will be part of a symphony, not a soloist."

I thought about what God was saying. "I'm not interested. I will be made a laughingstock in my community. Jews no longer accept prophets or prophesy. No modern Jew is a seer or a visionary. I'll be ridiculed and ostracized."

"Let's see if that's true," God said. In an instant, we were gone.

****

God took me into my past. When I was 25, I flew to Oregon to visit a cousin for the High Holy Days. She attended a small Conservative congregation in the Willamette Valley. The synagogue was not much bigger than a large two-story house. The sanctuary sat perhaps sixty people and was, as would be expected, packed for Yom Kippur. Even at the start of the day, the sanctuary's regular seats were full and a few of the folding chairs in the aisles were occupied. By the Yizkor service, it would be standing room only.

Outside the large, carved wooden doors leading to the sanctuary was a pile of shoes. A few in the community were poor and could not afford to purchase a pair of white canvas shoes only to be worn on Yom Kippur. The wealthier congregants abandoned their leather shoes before they entered the sanctuary, since wearing leather is prohibited on Yom Kippur. Those who wore tennis shoes that were not white took their shoes off, too. Even those who could afford new shoes went barefoot in solidarity with those with lesser means. The entire congregation was barefoot. I found it a delightful custom and smiled as I watched all the people sit at their seats in bare feet or wearing white socks. The lack of shoes made the whole event feel less formal, almost cozy. I had never been to a Yom Kippur service that was so homey. I was relaxed and felt welcome.

It was into this scene that God brought me. God and I stood behind the rabbi on the bimah, so I could see my younger self and everyone else in the room.

The congregation was about to sing *Avinu Malkeinu*, my favorite part of the liturgy during the High Holy Days. The younger version of me sang with the rest of the congregation, swaying with her eyes closed, her tallit covering her head. In Hebrew, she sang, "Our Father, Our King, be gracious. Answer our prayers, though we have little to commend us. Be kind and gentle with us, and save our people." She and the congregation sang the verse over and over until the depth of its meaning filled their hearts. The singing was so earnest and heartfelt that the entire room brightened. With a prophet's vision, I could see an angelic host gleaming through the windows on the sanctuary's north side. The angels, beams of light, raised their voices. Their chorus amplified the beauty of the human song.

The younger me felt the angels and trembled as she forgot herself and opened to the divine presence. It rushed through her. Her body went from imperceptible trembling to violent shaking. She sang, her body convulsing, though she remained standing. Although her eyes were closed, I could see the strain under her lids as her eyes rolled back in her head. She shuddered forcefully as her knees finally gave, and she fell to the ground. Fortunately, she was in the first row. She fell forward into the aisle in front of the bimah, and was not injured.

The young me lay on the floor, twitching, her eyes closed. It was difficult to separate myself from what I saw. I wanted to rush forward and help her, protect her, but I knew that I was unable to do anything. I was disembodied consciousness visiting another time and place. I also knew that she was in a state of rapture. But from the outside, she looked in distress, a small bit of drool coming from her mouth.

The scene also disgusted me. I looked at my younger self on the floor. She was helpless and vulnerable. I wanted her to take control of herself, to get up, and stop being a spectacle. I loved her, but she caused me to feel ashamed.

Two physicians, a nephrologist and an obstetrician, hurried to her side. "She's having a seizure," one of them said, moving back others who had come forward to assist.

I looked at God. "You see? They don't understand. If I'd been in a Pentecostal church, they would have recognized the experience for what it was, being 'slain in the spirit.' They would have asked me about my visions. These people are going to call an ambulance."

"You might have a point," God said.

"I most certainly do!"

"But you also have not been fair to these people. When you come to in a moment, when you are brought back by their actions to have your attention in this place, you will not tell them what happened. You will not share your experience with them. You will allow them to believe that you had a seizure. You will let the doctors in the hospital discharge you, perplexed that they can find no reason for what happened. You will be dishonest and, in keeping secrets, you do not give them the opportunity to grow."

I looked at the ground. "I still think they would have laughed at me."

"Maybe, and I am keeping that in mind, but perhaps not. Those who attend synagogue regularly or study Torah know the prophets. Every week in the synagogue, Jews read from the prophets. Others study them at home. While Jews as a whole may not believe that there are contemporary prophets, they do appreciate prophecy and the role of visionary experience in molding humankind's choices and experience."

I had not considered this and made no response. God continued, "Keep in mind too that I am not asking you to speak words of prophesy after a public visionary experience. I am not asking you to become some sort of missionary or preacher. I am asking you to write a story, a story you will tell as fiction, in which you can share truth. Is that not what good fiction is—truth dressed up in the trappings of a compelling story? Let people choose what they want to believe."

He appealed to the literature-lover part of me. "Sometimes," I said, "fictional tales can unquestionably feel as real and be as meaningful as lived existence. Dystopian works certainly are that, in their warnings about what could be. I'm reminded of the expression that what's true does not have to be real."

"Yes! Now you are beginning to understand," God said.

I remained unconvinced. "Maybe, but You allow Your prophets to look like fools. Look at all the flopping on the ground, trembling, and drooling. I want to be part of my community. There's no place in our contemporary tradition for seers and prophets. They're regarded either as charlatans or,"—I paused, looking for the right word—"schmendricks."

God laughed. "Perhaps." He paused. "I know what you must see next, Elinor."

Before we left the room, it was not to my younger self that I was drawn. I had no feelings for her now except embarrassment that I refused to allow into my heart. Instead, I turned to the windows on the north side of the building. There was no longer an amplification of light. When the congregation stopped singing to care for that younger version of me, the angels departed. The angelic choir has no desire to be near us when we stop singing God's praises.

****

We next arrived in the main sanctuary of a synagogue in Northern California. It was a beautiful chamber. The interior walls were built with large stone blocks that look like Jerusalem stone. The room gave the feeling of being at the

Kotel in Jerusalem. The shul was new, modern, and massive. The space was inspired.

I like contemporary synagogue construction that has a point of view. These fancy shuls were built in areas of the country where the Jews were wealthy and felt compelled to donate to the construction of beautiful places of worship, even if they did not regularly attend the synagogue or take an active part in synagogue life. This synagogue, built with Silicon Valley money, was meant to show the Jewish connection to Israel. Any Jew, Zionist or not, would feel at home.

I took my place with God on the balcony. We had a good view of the people below. This balcony was not built as a mechitza—the congregation was egalitarian—but as an overflow area for the High Holy Days. Below, a group of about a hundred people stood as the Torah was taken from the ark and paraded through the gathering.

"Your gifts are from Me, Elinor. Your visions are part of My work."

"You and I know that, but to the world, I'd be no more credible than a TV evangelist if I did what You asked."

I considered my conversations with God. They all take place in my head. Even though I feel like we are speaking, I know that the conversations are in another plane of existence, one in which telepathy is used. Some might ask how I know the difference between my own thoughts and God's. It's a good question.

There is a marked distinction. God's voice is concerned with others. It is kind and uplifting. The inner conversations I have with myself would deflate and discourage even the most optimistic individual. Anything that is self-centered or destructive I know comes from me. Words, especially those in defense of others, that build, warn, and heal—those are from God.

"That is why I am asking that you write for Me. You are known in the world as a writer. You can be framed simply as an artist if you use your gifts to write a book. Some will recognize the message in your work and be stirred to action. Those without that clarity may dismiss the work as dull or overly religious. Either way, you will be who and what you have always been—a storyteller."

A storyteller. I thought about what God said. I wasn't actually a writer in the world's eyes. My work, the work that paid the bills, was as a nonprofit executive. I created programs for women and girls, helping to build their skills and self-esteem and preparing them to be leaders in their communities. I had written a poetry book that received some awards and a book on nonprofit management that was an Amazon #1 bestseller, but I had not made the transition to writing as a career.

Writing was the work I had dreamed of in college. What I didn't know was how to make a living at it. When I lived in Los Angeles, I had taken up nonprofit work because it was fulfilling and highly regarded in my family. What I saw around me were a lot of out-of-work screenwriters who rarely seemed to finish or sell the scripts they perpetually worked on.

No, it wasn't reasonable to be a writer, my family reminded me. Few people could be like Margaret Atwood, Barbara Kingsolver, Stephen King, or J.K. Rowling, making a good income from writing. Writing, for someone like me, they proposed, was a hobby. If, in my spare time after all my obligations to work and family were complete, I could write that breakthrough hit, they would be pleasantly surprised. But writing could not take priority when there were cellphone bills and property taxes to be paid. If I was to be anything, it was responsible.

Yet here God was, in a sense, commanding me to follow my dreams and giving me a story to share. It was an important story, too, if I could get out of my own way to tell it.

I came back to what was in front of me as the Torah service started. The first reader commenced chanting from *B'reishit*. I felt the world around me begin to transform. The room twinkled, losing its solidness. The air conditioning's blast was replaced by a hot desert wind, and the façade of Jerusalem stone became the real thing. I listened more intently to the words from Torah, all the while feeling the heat, breathing in the distinct smell of sand and place that one only finds in the Middle East and North Africa. I realized that, without effort, I could understand the Hebrew, not a word here or there as usual, but all of it. I was not translating. I heard and understood the parsha in my soul. Sitting on the bench in my present, beside God in that synagogue, I was transported to Israel, to another place and time, while simultaneously being present in that shul.

I looked over in God's direction. He was no longer near, leaving me to the experience.

Reader after reader chanted from the Torah. The reading was parsha *Vayeira*, the section in which Sarah, at an advanced age, well beyond menopause, was told that she would have a child. She laughed at the news. She is challenged in the text, which asks her if anything is too wondrous for God to accomplish. Her response is to lie, denying that she laughed. She feared God. Then in the future, as it was foretold to her, she did have a son, Isaac, whom she would later learn was taken by her husband to be a sacrifice. She would die, perhaps of a broken heart, before Isaac's safe return.

Feeling Israel's hot climate while hearing Sarah's story, I was overcome with emotion. *Vayeira* is perhaps my least favorite parsha because, in a certain way, it tells my own story. It is unbearably painful to be unable to bear a child. Cosmic power, creation, God, the divine—in humans, that creative force comes through the female. We are born of women. God's manifestation in the world comes through the female of our species. I had never desired children, never wanted to raise a child, or have the experience of being a mother, but I felt completely devalued by my community because I could not have a child even if I wanted to.

But there was something I was clear about. God asked me to write a book, not have a baby. God asked me to give what I cared about most—stories—and what I was capable of producing. Was that not my version of giving birth?

I still felt dispirited. Alone on the balcony, where no one could see or hear me, I wept. When the Torah service concluded, I felt God's presence return beside me.

"There is a thin line between love and hate, God, and there are times that I hate You," I said. God said nothing, so I continued, "I drank for more than a decade, drank myself almost to death because I hated You as much as I loved You." God still said nothing. "How could You allow me to be useless, to be barren?"

"You're not useless," God said softly. "You write better than most, and your love for Me is matchless. I don't need you to have a baby. Many can have babies. But I do ask for something only you can create."

I stood up, turning on God. "Why did You bring me here?" I shouted. "You give me a beautiful gift of being able to feel Israel, to taste and see and smell our ancestral home, and then You ruin it by sharing the story of a barren woman who gets the one thing she wished for in life, a son, only to die of anguish when she learns that he has been taken as a sacrifice for You. What am I supposed to learn from that?" I was raging, screaming, and pounding my fists in the air. "I will never, ever have a child. No man in our community wants a woman like me, wants a woman who cannot give him a son. No one admires a woman who does not carry on our traditions by having children. I have no one to say *Kaddish* for me when I die. I am the last in my family line. My brother and my cousins are all intermarried. None have Jewish children." I paused, leaning toward God, hot tears running down my face. "You know how I became this dead end and You did nothing to stop it."

When I had finished my tirade, I fell to my knees. In the background, far away, I could hear the rabbi giving his d'var.

I felt what might have been a hand on my back, as if God had made Himself solid enough to give me comfort. "I brought you here to know that you are from a tremendous lineage and that while you will have no children of your own, that has no importance to Me. Your legacy is not to live through children, but from the words you share and the writings you use to teach. Your books are your legacy.

"Elinor, we are at the end of the generations, not because I will it, but because humankind collectively does not act for the benefit of those to come. I do not want you encumbered by children, making yourself upset over their dismal futures, dying because of what would become of them, as Sarah did. Because you are barren, because you are set apart from the world through your gifts, because of your particular talent to write, because of who you are in all your imperfection—all these traits and experiences are why you are, in My eyes, great and powerful. I favor you, Elinor. I love you. I love you as powerfully as you love Me."

I was too sad and tired to fight. I stood up. I didn't believe Him. How could He reciprocate my love? If He had, wouldn't He have been more generous? Wouldn't He have made my life easier? But I had no more energy to continue the challenge. "I have other concerns."

"We shall address them soon," God said, and let me return home.

****

Chapter Two

נחמו נחמו עמי יאמר אלהיכם

Comfort, comfort My people, says your God.

– Isaiah 40:1

It was three weeks before I spoke with God again. I felt Him around sometimes, His presence on the edge of my consciousness, but I ignored Him. I needed time and space to figure out my feelings. Assuming that God did want a broken and inconsequential person like me to speak for Him, to stand as a prophet and write what He asked of me, was I willing to do it?

I stood in the kitchen preparing spaghetti sauce. I don't care much for cooking, but I love making spaghetti sauce—probably because I love eating spaghetti. Oh boy, do I like spaghetti, though I wish I had a good recipe for kosher meatballs.

I had my containers of pre-chopped onions and pre-sliced, pre-washed mushrooms ready to go. While I washed the mushrooms, because I certainly don't trust that they're really as clean as they should be, I put the onions in a pan with olive oil, garlic, salt, pepper, and fresh Italian herbs. Once the mushrooms were washed and dried, I put them in with the

35

onions. I stood beside the stove, stirring occasionally until the vegetables were soft. Then I added diced tomatoes, more garlic, more herbs, halved cherry tomatoes, and my extra secret ingredient, a jar of premium pre-made sauce. Who has time to spend the whole day cooking down sauce? Once it was all bubbling together on a simmer, I added in the ground turkey I had cooked before starting to cook the vegetable portion of the sauce. The pan was, as always, filled right to the brim. I placed the lid on top and set the timer for forty-five minutes, breathing in deeply as I left the kitchen. The smell of pasta sauce filled the house.

Before I started cooking the pasta sauce, I had turned on the radio to a Canadian station that plays 'a mix of rock hits from the 1980s through today.' Pearl Jam. Foo Fighters. Our Lady Peace. Soundgarden. U2. Aerosmith. Red Hot Chili Peppers. And of course, a lot of The Tragically Hip.

As I sat on the couch to fold a heaping basket of laundry while the sauce simmered, "Comfortably Numb" by Pink Floyd came on the radio. I sat back, pushing the laundry basket away, really listening to the lyrics, even though I knew them by heart. I thought about how music can take us back to specific points in our lives. Then I thought about my life in particular. While the song is purported to be about a state of delirium the writer experienced in childhood, for me, it evokes memories of the choice I made to live my life despite the pain and trauma in my upbringing.

Trauma in childhood crushes the spirit. There are only a few ways to deal with it. One, and perhaps the most common, is to numb yourself. That might be through alcohol or drugs or mental illness. As I listened to "Comfortably Numb," I could imagine either using so many drugs that it's impossible to feel or going so deep inside yourself that you lose your connection to reality. I had done both earlier in my life. After years of suffering brutal, devastating abuse from my parents, I started drinking. I drank so much that I literally was unable to feel anything on a physical, emotional, or spiritual level. I also retreated from our shared reality, withdrew into myself, into fantasy, meditation, and visionary worlds. I would have died if I had continued, but when my parents suddenly and unexpectedly died one after the other when I was twenty-two, I made a different choice. Without my parents in my life, I had an opening to choose to live and be present in this world. When the guitar solo in the song began, I thought about the choice I had made to live this life to the fullest, to be engaged, even if that meant experiencing a great deal of pain.

What surprises many people is that I do not blame God for the difficulties of my past. I have always been quite aware of the fact that my parents were at the least mentally ill, if not overtly evil. I cannot believe that God intends cruelty to befall us. Certainly, we endure hardship. It is through misfortune and disease that humans grow spiritually. In these hardships, we are challenged to come together, to support one another, and to develop through our grief. Bad things do indeed happen to good people. None of us escapes that.

My challenge as a child was that I did not have a community to support me. I was left with people ill-suited to parenthood, far out in the country on a farm. Once I knew that I could not trust my parents, I did not know whom I could trust. My grandparents seemed impossibly old, and they lived hundreds of miles away. I spoke to them or saw them only a few times a year. My teachers seemed to report to my mother. As I grew older, I realized that their only assistance would

37

have been to pull me out of the home. That I did not want. As abusive as my parents were, I could not imagine living away from the farm and the animals that gave me strength. Plus, I'd found alcohol at an early age. Drinking, and feeling like I needed to protect and care for the animals, was what kept me going.

When the song finished, I was ready to speak to God again. Almost the moment I closed my eyes and prepared myself to call God, God was with me. God pulled me not to our regular meeting place at the fallen tree beside the meadow, but to a Sikh temple I had once visited in New Delhi.

The Gurudwara Bangla Sahib is a palatial structure near Connaught Circle, a short walk from my hotel. On that visit, I was a sophomore in college. My university study abroad group had arrived the previous morning and stayed awake as long as possible. I made it until just after 4 p.m.

The next morning, we were awakened before dawn and taken to the Sikh temple. It was a magnificent sight. The marble and gold shone in the sun's first rays. I had the same feeling of awe on this occasion as I had had on my first visit.

God waited for me. He stood, if you can call it that, outside the temple's entrance, where people leave their shoes. One doesn't wear shoes at Sikh holy sites.

I smiled as I looked at the entry. "Why are we at this place?"

God took a moment before He answered. "You don't believe that you are enough. What you see in the mirror is an illusion, a warped picture that comes from your parents' shortcomings. That is a tragedy and a mistake. I want you to see yourself the way I see you, the way most of the rest of the world sees you. I want you to feel that you are special. You are gifted and talented. Others see greatness. That is what I see and that is why you were chosen for this task."

The sun had begun to rise. Coming in our direction was a small group of American university students, clearly out of place in the throng of Sikhs. A younger version of me was among them, not quite nineteen years old. She was heavier than anyone else in the group, though not nearly as big as I remembered. She was sturdy. She had ridden horses all summer, taking care of a small herd at a Girl Scout camp in the mountains just north of Los Angeles. She wore a long cotton skirt, tan and white with a swirling pattern, a black cotton t-shirt, and brown suede Arizona-style Birkenstocks. The skirt I still have, though the shoes became so worn and smelly after this trip that I had to throw them away when I got home. Her nose was pierced with a small faux diamond stud. A friend from camp had shoved it through the skin when they were all drunk on a break in a park. Along with the other students, that younger version of me handed her shoes to an attendant and pulled a shawl out to place over her head before going into the courtyard. God and I followed.

Before entering the worship hall, the students and worshippers washed their hands and feet. I smiled as the Americans awkwardly tried to mimic the deft actions of the Sikhs. Jason, a bright young man from Pennsylvania, began to ask questions of a Sikh man who had welcomed him in English. The man was friendly and open. The other students gathered around to listen to what the man said. They had not been prepped to visit a Sikh temple. I smiled to myself, thinking about all the reading I had done over the summer before this trip, learning about Hindu gods and goddesses— and feeling hopelessly lost when my first experience of

39

religion in India was this visit to a Sikh temple. I was completely unprepared and had no idea what I was looking at or about to experience.

The students followed the man toward the main hall. God and I continued to move with the group.

The hall filled quickly, and the younger me became separated from the rest of the group. She stood in a lavish space. Everything seemed to be sparkling gold or polished marble. People pushed forward, but in a calm, rather than menacing way. This was not a mob. Still, as the young woman was pressed toward the front of the hall, toward what can best be described as an altar area with a large, extravagant canopy, she became visibly frightened. She gazed right and left, scanning the room for any sight of her group, but she found no one. Meanwhile, the assembly became increasingly squeezed as people packed into the room to see the Guru Granth Sahib, the Great Book, brought to its daytime resting place by a magnificent procession.

The woman, nearly frantic, didn't notice an elderly Sikh couple approaching her from behind until they were in front of her, facing her. She towered over them, an imposing figure at least eight inches taller than either of them. They were bent and slight, both wearing thin white cotton clothes, greyed from time and washing. The elderly woman began to speak earnestly to the younger woman, but could not make herself understood. Having only been in the country a few hours, the younger woman had no idea even which language was being spoken, let alone what the older woman was trying to communicate.

The older woman, seeing that the American did not understand, looked at her husband and smiled warmly. They then both bent down in front of the young American and began to chant something, not quite in unison, while they reached forward and touched her feet. The young woman looked down at them, a look of shock and disbelief on her face. Then, not knowing what to do, she squealed in panic, leaped over the two elderly people, shoved her way through the crowd, and ran out the back door into an enormous courtyard with a reflecting pool in it.

At the reflecting pool, she saw part of her group, including the professor. They sat together, gazing at the water and chatting. She ran toward them.

"What happened?" the professor asked. He was a tall and lanky middle-aged man with thin, greying hair. He'd gone to India a month before the students and had caught an intestinal bug that had left him lethargic. He'd lost twenty pounds and was already punching holes in his belt to tighten it.

God and I followed the young woman out and listened attentively as she described to the professor what had happened. I smiled, remembering that because I had no idea what the elderly couple was doing, I had felt like they were preparing me for—I don't know what. Maybe something sinister? That didn't feel true, but I didn't understand them. Their earnestness and softness scared me as they gently touched my feet, muttering what I assumed were prayers.

The professor shook his head, pressing his hands to his eyes and covering a half smile. "Elinor, they were blessing you," he said quietly. "The feet are the dirtiest part of the body. You have heard of people washing one another's feet? The Pope does it sometimes. The highest figure in the Catholic church washes the feet of the poor and homeless. It's a sign of humility for the foot-washer and honor for the

41

washed." He paused. When the woman gave no reply, he continued, "They were acknowledging you as someone special."

The young woman looked shocked. She said nothing for at least half a minute. I knew what she was thinking. She had never been recognized in any meaningful way, at least not by her family. When she had earned her Girl Scout Gold Award, her mother hadn't been interested in going to the ceremony. She was the only one there without a parent. Her father didn't attend her bat mitzvah or high school graduation. When she and her partner were in the high school debate finals at the state competition, which took place at the local community college only twenty minutes from her house, her mother didn't even ask what time the round was. She had been left home to take care of the animals when her family had gone on vacation to Mexico. No matter how she succeeded or what she accomplished, her parents didn't care. Being viewed as somehow special was an entirely novel experience.

I thought about this as I looked at her standing there, frightened and almost in shock. This younger version of myself had been beaten down by life and her family to such a point that she could not in any way conceive of herself as having value. She felt broken and tainted. It was impossible for her to imagine that she was worthy of blessing. I looked over at God, saddened by this view of a person I had once been. Then I turned my back on this scene and closed my eyes, wishing that I didn't have to witness this part of my life anymore.

****

Our next stop was high in the Indian Himalayas, outside a Buddhist monastery. God and I arrived ahead of the student group. I knew they would be along soon.

These were Tibetan Buddhists of the Dalai Lama's order. They had fled to India to escape the Chinese occupation of Tibet. The small monastery was about an hour and a half drive from the main Tibetan refugee settlement in Dharamsala. The building was set back in the forest, surrounded by tall conifers. It was misty and cool, reminding me in many ways of my home in the Pacific Northwest. I took in the forest smell—trees, damp, mist, earth—and smiled. The forest, any temperate forest, is my favorite place to be.

The building's façade was plain. It seemed to be made of or covered with some type of mud or clay, and was painted white with a simple yellow-gold trim. The building was far humbler than other Tibetan structures, which sometimes had finely carved roofs and bright ornamentation. There were no windows on our side of the building. The location looked deserted. While we waited for people to arrive, God and I had an opportunity to talk.

"That Sikh couple saw something special in you, Elinor," God said. "Just as I do."

I said nothing. I couldn't for the life of me think what that 'specialness' might be. In my estimation, I'm an average woman. I have my strengths and my shortcomings. I'm not conventionally beautiful or stylish. I'm clumsy and have a short temper. I have a tendency to be bossy and I am loud. I am also wicked smart, witty, and adventurous. I am a great storyteller. My friends find me loyal and attentive. I am generous. My moral compass guides my actions most of the time. I feel like I see myself fairly clearly, the good and bad.

Yet to be a prophet, to speak for God, shouldn't one be in some way exceptional? Shouldn't I be a tzadik? Isn't the lowest qualification for this calling to be a spiritual master? I don't even keep kosher. How could God possibly believe I am up to the task?

"Not convinced?" God asked, less a question than a statement. "I want you to believe in this project. I want you to believe in yourself so that you will be able to follow through with the task and the fallout."

"Does it matter what I think of myself or what I want?" I asked. "Jonah didn't want the job. Neither did Moses. Aaron and Miriam got nothing but difficulties from doing what You asked. Why would I want to sign up?"

"No, they did not want to volunteer," God said softly. He paused, seemingly measuring His words. "I want you to believe that the action is necessary. If after all I will show you, you do not believe humankind needs to change and has at least a tiny chance of heeding the call for social transformation, then there is no hope for change. If after showing you miracles and visions, you are not willing to change, how could I expect you to convince others that the status quo is not OK?" God paused again. "I need you to believe that even with your faults, you are special, and that because of these imperfections, you bring something extraordinary to the role of prophet."

"Yes, but I am not exceptional, I—"

God interrupted. "You have come through harrowing circumstances and situations and continue to love and be devoted to Me. It is your charm and tenacity that will allow you to change the world."

As God finished speaking, two elderly monks came around the back side of the building to meet a minibus making its way slowly up the road from the south. "And whatever you might say about yourself, My dear Elinor, you are incomparable."

The bus pulled to a stop beside the building. The monks, in deep red robes accented with yellow, stood waiting to greet the students. Their hands were pressed together in front of them, their faces calm.

The university students—the same group that had been at the Sikh temple in New Delhi—tumbled from the bus in noisy jubilation. They seemed pleased to put their shoes on the ground after a slow and stressful journey through the mountains. The young people laughed and joked, bumping into one another as they jostled off the bus. Their joviality was a stark contrast to the monks' calm. None of them seemed to notice the monks until they were all off the bus and, like a herd of calves ready to move from barn to pasture, they skipped and crowded in the direction of the monastery's entrance. The sight of the monks, however, stopped them cold. They immediately remembered themselves, put their hands together almost in unison, and bowed politely before their hosts.

Without a word, they were taken around the corner to the building's entrance. There was a row of metal prayer wheels opposite the building. Each wheel was about two feet tall and covered in Sanskrit. Though I could not read the words, I guessed they said, "Om Mani Padme Hum," which is the traditional prayer most often associated with these wheels. Buddhists will circumambulate prayer wheels, spinning them in the belief that they receive merit for doing so, no different than if they had recited the prayer. The wheels are beautiful. Although man-made, they fit in with their natural surroundings. Their sanctity enhanced the natural splendor of the forest. Without them, the place would have been somehow diminished.

As each of the students removed their shoes and filed quietly inside, they let out a tiny gasp. The building's interior was as lavish and luxuriant as the exterior was plain. The ceiling was divided into squares, each painted in vivid reds, oranges, greens, yellows, and blues. The pillars were made of carved wood, also painted brightly with designs such as dragon's heads, clouds, and flowers. The floor was polished wood that shone from careful buffing. There were tapestries on the walls depicting Buddhas and otherworldly creatures. At the front of the meditation room was an altar with a large golden Buddha statue surrounded by dozens of smaller statues. In front of the altar was an array of items: fruit, flowers, candles, and luxurious fabrics. A wide-seated chair and a hand drum were beside the altar.

Once all the students had entered the meditation hall, a monk came into the room from another entrance and took his seat on the chair. He sat in it cross-legged. He was wizened, old beyond guessing, with a great toothless smile. He beckoned for the students to come into the center of the room and seemed to indicate with a gentle swish of his hand for them to be seated.

The students sat in three rows of six. They were mixed by gender, two women, two men, two women, in each row. The old monk on the chair laughed. The students stared at him expectantly.

A younger monk, probably in his seventies, stepped forward. He too smiled graciously at the students. In thickly accented English, he said, "You welcome here. I speak little bit English." He pinched his fingers close together to indicate that his English skills were indeed minimal. "Today, we practice Buddhist meditation. You sit cross-legs like him," the monk said, pointing at the old man in the chair. "No point feet at anyone. Very rude."

I looked at the younger me. She had known that she would be expected to sit on the floor, so she had worn loose-fitting blue cotton pants and her favorite baggy black sweater. She sat in the back row on the end nearest the door, looking earnest, but uncomfortable. I knew that if she sat cross-legged long enough, her legs would start to go to sleep. Without a cushion, the pressure on her tailbone would be immense, and she'd start to hurt within a few minutes. Nonetheless, she crossed her legs, tucked her toes under her as best she could, straightened her back, and gave her complete attention to the monks.

"We soon close eyes and focus on breath. Deep breath in. Slow breath out." He and the monk in the chair demonstrated. Once it was clear that the students knew what to do, everyone except the English-speaking monk closed their eyes and began the meditation practice. The monk who was not participating in the meditation went to the back of the room and observed.

The younger version of me looked as calm as the other students for the first two or three minutes. After that, it became clear that she was uncomfortable sitting cross-legged. She lifted her tailbone from the floor by leaning forward slightly. Half a minute later, she wiggled her backside from left to right.

Two minutes after that, she opened her eyes and quietly uncrossed her legs, stretching her right leg out in front of her and moving her foot back and forth. She then put it back. Not a minute later, she stretched her other leg. Defeated, she stretched her legs in front of her, crossed them at the ankles, and leaned forward toward the floor. It was obvious that she was not going to be able to complete the meditation.

Soundlessly, the English-speaking monk walked up behind her. He tapped her gently on the shoulder. When she turned, he motioned for her to follow him. She did so as quietly as she could. Looking around as she left the hall, she noticed that all the other students were still, involved in their meditation practice.

The young woman and the monk both put on their shoes and walked to the prayer wheels, the monk in the lead, the woman a few steps behind. The monk turned and smiled at the young woman. "You no good meditation. Maybe learn meditate next life," he said and laughed. She smiled, embarrassed. Then the monk got more serious. "You very special person," he continued, pointing his bony finger toward her heart. She smiled awkwardly. "You no Buddhist. No Christian, too."

"No," she replied. "I am Jewish." She wondered if he knew what a Jew was.

"Yes," he said, smiling. "Dalai Lama say good to practice religion of birth." He paused. His face and tone grew more earnest. "You are, they say, touched by God. You get big blessing today."

The woman smiled self-consciously. She didn't understand what he was trying to say. What did it mean to be 'touched' by God? At home, the expression meant that one was crazy, but she knew the monk would never say anything as ungracious as that. And what was the 'big blessing' that she would receive?

The monk gave her little time to ponder these questions. He began to circumambulate the prayer wheels, spinning them as he went. The woman had seen this done before, in a film on Tibetan Buddhism she had been shown during her orientation session on India. Because the students were attending a language school high in the Indian Himalayas, the faculty in charge of the program suspected that they would encounter Tibetan refugees living in India. Knowing something about their situation and traditions was essential for preparing the students for their trip.

After one round of slow, purposeful circumambulation, the monk stopped before the woman. "You turn wheels, but run. You not go slow like me. Run fast."

The woman looked at him as if he'd gone mad. She'd been removed from the meditation session because she was too big to sit comfortably on the floor. Now she was being asked to run at goodness-only-knew what ridiculous elevation. They were not at the tree line, but pretty close to it. What was that in the Himalayas? At least six thousand feet, she speculated. This was not quite the easiest place for a large woman to run and get a good lungful of air.

Unwilling to argue with her host, she did as she was asked. She ran slowly around the prayer wheels in the direction he had indicated, spinning them with her right hand as she did. She ran around twice, three times, four. The monk disappeared, going back inside the building. The woman continued to run, faster than she thought she could. She ran for more than twenty minutes, the whole while thinking about nothing. It was a relief not to have racing thoughts, not to fly into another reality, especially not to hear from God. She was simply there, alone, in the moment, spinning the prayer wheels.

While she ran, God spoke to Elinor. "That monk recognized you. He singled you out as someone special."

Elinor looked incredulously at God. "What are You talking about?" she asked. "He pulled me out of the meditation because I couldn't sit still. I was a disruption."

God countered quickly, "Do you think that there isn't at least one person in every group that visits here who cannot sit still? Do you think that while you might have been the first in that group to get uncomfortable, you were the only one who fidgeted? Come on, Elinor. You knew those kids in the room. They weren't going to be able to meditate any better than you did."

"He told me that I could learn to meditate in my next life," Elinor quipped. "That indicates a pretty dim view of my potential."

"He told you that your path is not like the others. You have special blessings, and to cultivate those blessings, you have to follow a different path. He pulled you out of that room to give you access to a different form of activity. Through giving you a repetitive action, running around the prayer wheels, he helped you access an altered state of consciousness. When is your brain ever silent? When can you run continuously for the better part of a half-hour? You were in an altered state that allowed your mind and body to function in different ways

50

from their norm. He pulled you out to train your mind precisely for the task I am setting before you."

God's comments gave me pause. I wordlessly continued to watch my younger self circumambulate the prayer wheels. 'Is that what an altered state looks like from the outside?' I wondered silently to myself. The young woman was robust and acted purposefully, without fatigue. She also had a blank look in her eye, not of nothingness, but of being somewhere else. Yes, maybe God was onto something here. Maybe this activity would have taught her more than sitting uncomfortably in a meditation room. I considered this way of viewing events until God took us from the scene.

****

God and I arrived in the Kalahari, a semi-arid, sandy savannah that covers parts of Namibia, Botswana, and northern South Africa. I looked around for ants or snake trails and, seeing none, plopped down on the ground. God's shimmer made itself smaller beside me, as if God too sat. I said nothing, taking in a deep breath of the cool, clean air and looked out toward the horizon. In front of us was a small herd of twenty-five or so springbok. The animals are delicate, with thin bones and white faces and underbodies. They seem fragile, like good china, but they are in fact swift and hardy creatures that are able to make their way in an unforgiving land.

I had been here once before, when I was thirty-six. I had come with a tour an associate of mine led. He was a writer and anthropology professor. He wrote popular books about the spiritual practices of people in remote areas of the world.

Spiritual seekers, would-be yogis, the wayward and lost—if they had the money—could go with him to visit the traditional healers he wrote about. This year, we were with the San.

The San, also known as the Bushmen of the Kalahari, are potentially the oldest population of human beings on Earth. They are hunter-gatherers who live in small kinship groups. They are petite in stature, generally light-colored for people with darker skin-tones, with a suggestion of honey or yellow hues. They have long been persecuted by other ethnic groups and colonial authorities. However, after being mythologized in the film *The Gods Must be Crazy*, wealthy and often sad Westerners will pay large sums to guides who can introduce them to the groups' spiritual healers.

"I am glad that You brought me here in winter," I said, half to myself. In July, the desert was pleasantly warm during the day and cold at night. In my opinion, winter was by far the most enjoyable time of year. This time of day, just before dusk, set my heart ablaze with gratitude and hope. Maybe I had more to offer than I realized. The sand beneath my bottom was still warm from the day's sun. I smiled.

"Do you understand yet how special you are, Elinor?" God asked.

"I'm not really sure what that means," I said, continuing to watch the springbok graze. I thought about dinner. I had eaten springbok once at a fancy restaurant in Cape Town. It was far too gamey in flavor for my liking. I laughed to myself, knowing that the springbok, while a delicious treat to a San hunter, would always be safe from me.

"Don't you?" God asked. I shook my head. God waited at least a full minute before He continued. "There are certain people, like the shaman and prophet, the visionary and seer, who have an ability to open themselves to higher levels of consciousness. That is where you find Me."

I listened intently. God went on, "You have a capacity for expanded consciousness that is broader than almost anyone else on the planet. Part of that is simply who you are. Part of it comes from your devotion to Me and your great compassion for other living beings."

I held my hand up. "Come on now. I don't know if that's true. Aren't you exaggerating a bit?"

"What about the rabbit?"

I put my hand down. Earlier in the week, I was on my way to the barn where I board my horse. Just before the turnoff, I saw the body of a rabbit in the center of the road. I began to say a silent prayer, as I generally do when I see roadkill. I can't imagine how awful it must be to lose one's life in that way, and so I say a prayer that begins with the *Shema* and continues with a request for blessing for the animal's soul. As I sped past, however, I saw in the rearview mirror that the animal had lifted up its head. It was not dead.

Unable to leave the rabbit on the road, I turned around and went back. Let me assure you that I am not a brave person, and if I had to kill my own food, I would be a vegetarian. There was no way that I could dispatch the rabbit. Even so, I could not leave it to suffer. I imagined the rabbits in *Watership Down*, their fear of anything with an engine, and I thought of that rabbit lying there, injured, with cars whizzing past. No, I could not leave it. I put my car in park, turned on the hazards, and got out to investigate.

The rabbit was young and thin, probably born earlier in the year. However, the way it lay outstretched indicated a probable spinal injury and possibly other internal problems. I didn't know what to do. I reached out and stroked it, standing over it as other cars went by. If I left, it would most likely only be a matter of minutes before the rabbit was crushed.

When there was a break between the cars passing, I went back to my car to get a cotton grocery bag. I was afraid to pick the rabbit up, afraid that I would make its injuries worse. A woman pulled up in a car behind me and got out of her vehicle, but did not offer to help. Another car pulled off the road behind her. They all waited for me to take action.

An older woman, at least sixty, came upon the scene in the opposite lane. She was in a black SUV that had recently been washed. Her hair was long and silver. She was thin, with a fast smile. "Do you need help?" she asked, seeing the rabbit.

"Yes," I replied. "I saw this rabbit here. It has been hit, but I can't leave it in the street."

"Pick it up by the back legs," she offered.

"I think it has a spinal injury," I said.

"Would you like me to pick it up for you?" she asked softly. "Put it in the bag?"

"Thank you," I said. "I'm not very brave about these things."

She laughed. "Well, I am an ER nurse." She scooped the rabbit up gently in the middle and placed it carefully in the grocery bag. "We can handle situations like this."

"Thank you," I said, my gratitude clear in my voice.

"What will you do with it?" she asked.

"I'll take it to my barn and put it in a safe place under the brambles. Either it's stunned and will get up, or it's too far gone and will pass somewhere comfortable, where it doesn't have to be afraid."

The woman nodded, got into her car, and drove away. I took the rabbit the quarter-mile or so to my barn, where a friend took it gently to the blackberry bushes where the rabbits love to hide, and left it alone to live out the final moments of its life in the shade.

"How many cars went past you? Eight? Ten? Elinor, you were the one with the open heart. That's quite an asset that not everyone has."

I contemplated this perspective as God continued, "You are a unique combination of broken down and broken open. You have endured enough hardships to demonstrate that resilience and change are possible, no matter how challenging. At the same time, you are not bitter or hardened by your experiences."

"I am hard, God," I said, interrupting. "Friends have always criticized me for not showing enough vulnerability."

"You are competent and manage your life. You're not a child or a flower that needs to be protected. What is it that your friend's husband said to you recently?"

"That I am not the kind of woman men want to date, but I am exactly the kind of woman a man knows he wants to marry and be in partnership with after he has dated or married the wrong ones."

"From that, I would deduce that rather than thinking you need to be more vulnerable, you should perhaps lead a bit more with your fun side."

I smiled. "I think my sense of adventure might be a little too much for most guys." God and I both laughed. Here we were, sitting in the Kalahari watching a herd of springbok and talking about changing the world. That's not the kind of life most people lead nor is it the kind of life conducive to partnership. Who wants to play second fiddle to God?

"Yes, Elinor, to do as I want, you are going to have to give up some of your ideas—stories you tell yourself about a 'normal' life with a husband, children, and a mortgage. But you've never wanted that, not really. It's what you think you *should* want. Yes, people will ridicule you and some will inappropriately follow you, but you have no control over any of that. What I am asking is that you step forward, into your authority, and use your talents to give your species and this planet a real shot at an abundant life."

Instantly, we moved to a new location. We stood beside a campfire in what had been my group's Namibian base camp. Around the fire in a three-quarter crescent were about thirty San, mostly women, and children. The younger men were away hunting. Only two older men were in the camp. The whole community sang, harmonizing and clapping in quick, staccato rhythms. Two elderly women, shamans, danced around the fire. They moved with short, pounding steps. Although beautiful, the dance, clapping, and singing were discordant. Each part was a counterpoint to the others, which created an otherworldly effect. Time seemed to stop. Space shifted. In a short time, the shamans' facial expressions changed. Their features went slack and their eyes became wide and black. They turned their heads left and right, as if seeing things not present in our shared reality.

A San shaman works with an energy they call n/om. The energy is equivalent to the Chinese concept of *qi*, activated in the bodies of the healers. As the shaman dances, she turns on a sort of motor in the center of her belly. The energy there is hot. Using the dance, the shaman intensifies and heats up the n/om, pushing it through the heart and out the crown of the head. In this altered state, the healer undergoes a transformation and is awakened. It can be an uncomfortable transition, but it connects the healer to the healing power of the community and the ancestors.

I watched the two shamans reach this altered state in which they danced and danced until they screamed and laughed. They put their hands in the fire, but were not burned. They sweat beyond imagining. Eventually, one would throw the other into the dirt and use it to cool her.

Only after they had been in this state for some time, did they turn their attention to the Americans. On the bottom of the crescent stood the small group of eight travelers my colleague had brought to Namibia. My heart broke for so many of them. They suffered from depression, anxiety, or lack of direction. Two were ill, one chronically, the other terminally. All sought a fast path to enlightenment. They wanted results without putting in the effort. Though each was financially well-off, their lives were small, and they knew it.

These oversized pilgrims—even the most petite was nearly twice the size of the average San—raised their arms high over their heads, as if in an Evangelical tent revival. They swayed with the music, their eyes closed. When the shamans came around to them, they fell to the ground. The shamans jumped out of the way to keep from being crushed. Once on the ground, the Americans writhed and shook. The shamans ran their hands over these fallen people, trying to remove or align 'arrows' that cause sickness or create energetic blocks. The shamans trembled, washing their hands in the fire, then returning to their work. They leaned over the Americans, sucking and pulling energetic arrows and evil from them. As they worked, the shamans groaned and shouted. The spectacle was irresistible.

The thirty-six-year-old me sat in a chair behind the eldest woman in the circle. The elder was close to the fire and served not only as a buffer between the Americans and the San, but seemed to be somehow in charge, or at least keeping an eye on things. At one point, through an interpreter, she told my colleague to tell the Americans to stop falling down. They had to either stand or sit in the dirt like everyone else, but the falling was unacceptable.

I couldn't quite understand all the falling. I think it had to do with cultural expectations. The San were healed while seated. I think the Americans thought they would be 'slain in the spirit,' knocked over by the overwhelming presence of the divine. Because of this expectation, they fell over when the shamans laid their hands upon them. At least, that was my hypothesis.

Healing dances last the whole night. This was no exception. For hours, the shamans circled through the Americans, who pushed to get in front of one another, to get a little more n/om. The younger me watched, fascinated. How could one believe themselves to be in an altered state, she wondered of the Americans, and also be conscious and selfish enough to push others aside to get another dose of feel-good energy? I knew there were no shortcuts to spiritual development.

Without warning, the two shamans turned away from the standing Americans and grabbed the younger me. She had been greatly affected by the music and dancing, her own n/om wildly awakened inside. The shamans seized her hands roughly and drew her from her camp chair. Pulling her past the eldest woman, they took her to the center of the group, close to the fire. She grunted and groaned as she, too, began to tremble like the shamans. The shamans moved their hands over her. Unlike the other Americans, she did not raise her arms in delight or fall to the ground. She stood against the ever-quickening energy in her body, her feet firmly planted on the earth.

To those in a trance, the n/om was discernible as heat and light. Like a serpent jetting up her spine, the younger me felt the n/om shoot through the top of her head. She groaned as she saw around her strings of light, ladders that promised to take her to distant destinations. She stayed put, focusing on grounding the energy in her trembling legs, despite the heat rising and violent shaking, the sweat running down her face and back, pooling under her breasts. The shamans pulled on her, urging her into the dirt. Once there, they drew the excess energy from her with their hands and used the dirt to wick the heat away.

Although the shamans did not speak any English, they communicated with her in flashes of light and pictures. What they said made no sense linguistically, but she understood the message perfectly; the shamans recognized her as a seer and healer. She was being acknowledged not as extraordinary, but for the gifts she had to share with others. They also were concerned that her uterus was stone cold, dead. No amount of heat or healing directed at it would ever allow her to bear children.

The former she appreciated. The latter, she intuitively knew and thanked them for their concern. *It was OK*, she told them. She didn't have the right personality to be a mother.

As suddenly as they had grabbed her, the shamans turned away. They went back into the center of the group near the fire where the chanting and clapping had reached a fever-pitch. The woman lay on the ground, exhausted, as the sun's first rays began to peek over the horizon. The music stopped. The San quietly got up and walked back to their camp. One of the cooks tended the fire. The Americans shuffled off to bed. Only my younger self remained lying on the ground, spiritually drunk, watching the stars repattern themselves into a herd of springbok that jumped along the sky.

****

God returned me to my home. The pasta sauce still simmered on the stove, the depth of the aroma telling me it was done. The clothes I had been folding remained in the laundry basket. I opened my eyes slowly to find myself sitting cross-legged on the couch, as if in meditation.

I got up gently, making my way to the kitchen. I turned the stove off, took a glass from the shelf, and from the refrigerator, got myself some water. I gulped it down and refilled the glass. From the pantry, I grabbed an oversized chocolate bar with nuts. That, with a third glass of water, I took back to the couch. I ate hungrily. Visionary experience and spiritual travel leave me famished.

God's shimmer was in the white barrel chair to my right. He waited patiently, understanding that I had to attend to my physical needs before I could speak with Him. I wondered as I ate the chocolate what God's experience of people is like. Are we like beloved pets to Him? How does He feel about us? I imagined that it was not something I would understand, so I did not give voice to the question. I knew that God could read my mind, but He chose not to provide an answer. Perhaps He too knew that the response would be unfathomable to a being of flesh with its consciousness constrained by the architecture and chemistry of the brain.

When I was done with my candy bar and most of the third glass of water, I looked in God's direction. I was cold and pulled a throw blanket from my right, wrapping myself in it.

God spoke first. "Why, Elinor, when you have had these extraordinary experiences with holy people around the world, do you still refuse to believe that you are special? The relationship that you have with Me is a tremendous gift. Are you unable to see that?"

"So many of the people I know of or have read about who call themselves prophet, visionary, or shaman are frauds. Some are well-meaning, but overconfident in their abilities. Others are self-aggrandizing. Still, others simply love the money they can bilk out of people. More times than not, they have a combination of these features. I don't want any of those mantles. I don't seek fortune or fame or a following for the spiritual gifts I have. If I do what You ask, how can I know that I won't be put into the category of fraud?"

"I hope your feelings will become rooted more in humility and less in shame. And since prophecy, in this era, can only be told as fiction, then that is how it will be written. What if we do not begin the story in the traditional way," God said, "with thunder and lightning and Me and the angels on a mountaintop somewhere? What if we begin the story with you, the reluctant mystic who is first and foremost a human being? You are a Jewish woman who struggled with alcohol and makes great pasta sauce. You have cats, but no children.

You are kind-hearted to the injured, human or otherwise. You enjoy riding your horse. You are a talented writer who has had the good fortune to travel the world. Your exceptional love and openness to Me allow you to experience a kind of reality few others have access to. This causes you embarrassment. The wise will see the truth behind the story. They will have no interest in you as the messenger. They will have interest only in the message."

"No one will listen, God. Most people want more, to be the chief glutton in the piggish game of overconsumption. People don't seem to be looking for revelation, but for status, money, and possessions. We have created a society in which material wealth is most prized, not connection, community, and growth."

"You might be right, Elinor," God said. "People rarely change their ways, though you did. You quit drinking. Each being has free will and so it is possible, just possible, that humankind will change. What is that saying? That you are spiritual beings having a physical experience. If we can help humankind to remember that, to place community and connection before materialism and gain, there is hope."

I shook my head. How could God know us so well and not know us at all?

God's shimmer expanded and brightened. He had read my mind. "That is something about which for now, we will have to agree to disagree. I always have hope," God said, and disappeared.

****

62

Chapter Three

אליכם אישים אקרא וקולי אל־בני אדם

O men, I call to you. My cry is for all humankind.
– Proverbs 8:4

As I made myself comfortable to watch the election results come in, my mind wandered back to the first election I could remember, Jimmy Carter's 1980 reelection bid. I was eight. I sat on the floor in front of the television while my dad lay on the couch. Our family TV had a small screen, maybe fifteen inches, nothing like the giant screens we have today. That it was color was a genuine treat. My parents had recently splurged on a new television set, putting the old black-and-white in their bedroom. On the screen was a map of the United States. I didn't understand what was happening at all. The 'TV show' seemed to have no discernible plot, just a news anchor reading off numbers. Eventually, the results were in. President Carter had lost, and we were going to have a new president, Ronald Reagan. Too young to understand things like the Iran hostage crisis or the bombing of the Marine barracks in Lebanon, what I did comprehend was that the smiling, kind man we saw so often on the evening news was going away. I cried. Even now, I retain that childhood fondness for President Carter and his pleasant, reassuring grin.

I sat back against a pile of pillows, one of my cats lying down beside me. On my lap, my laptop lay open. The polls would soon close in the East. I started to feel pulled toward a vision, but I didn't need a visionary experience to know what the results would be. I felt it in my body, and it made me ill.

The man who was soon to be elected was dangerous. He'd already been the cause of calamitous events that nearly toppled the federal government, and the judicial process was too slow and compromised to keep him from returning to power. Still, God wanted me to see what was to come.

I refused the vision. I didn't want to see. The possibilities were too ugly and hit too close. There was so much at stake in this election that it was difficult for me to accept that 'my side' would lose.

Around the nation, progressives held their breath. Would we win and continue years of reform? Would we expand medical care to more Americans, finally getting the single-payer system so many of us wanted? Would women continue to make gains, receiving the right to paid maternity leave, and others to family leave? Would the LGBTQ community breathe easier knowing that their hard-won right to marriage would be protected? Would the new president continue to invest in NASA and our space program, in learning more about our cosmos and the planets around us, as well as our own weather systems? Would we continue our fight against cancer, diabetes, heart disease, HIV, and other healthcare issues by investing in medical research? Would those with addiction or mental health issues find greater access to effective, compassionate treatment? Would we make important efforts to reverse climate change? If our candidate won, we expected a resounding, "Yes!" to each of those questions, with legislation and funding to follow. But victory was not assured. I sat glued to the computer, hoping against hope that my intuition was wrong.

The first polls closed in the East. I put down a bowl of extra-buttered popcorn and turned on the TV. The expected states went our way: New York, Massachusetts, Vermont. The margins were great. My friends began to celebrate. They sent messages exhorting our victory. I did not join in the festivities. Other states didn't come in quickly. I leaned forward, concerned. The results were closer in Florida and Virginia. While my friends celebrated victory, my heart sank. I told them via text to stop their parties and pay attention to the news. We were not going to have an easy victory, and we just might lose.

The truth was I had already felt the loss. I had felt it earlier in the week, a knowing in my core. The phrase, "It's the economy, stupid," kept playing over and over in my mind. We were not going to win this one. Just like how I knew which horse would win the Derby, I knew the outcome of this election, had felt it for days, but could not allow myself to believe it. It was the 'too close to call' race in Virginia that confirmed what I felt. I live-streamed election results on my computer while I listened to the network commentators on TV. "No path to victory" was the consensus about five hours later. We had lost.

The backlash against Jews was immediate. Though the inflamed rhetoric of the president-elect was against Muslims, it is Jews who are the low-hanging fruit for ethnic hatred. We are historically cast in false narratives as being nefarious characters controlling the media and banks, making us both evil and a threat. Within hours of the election, the violence began. There were attacks at synagogues and Jewish community centers in New Jersey, Florida, Pennsylvania, Louisiana, and California. Rabbinical schools in New York and California were vandalized, then burned. Over the next few weeks, many of my friends fled, especially those most vulnerable in the South and small towns. Some went to larger cities. Others moved to Israel. A few went to Canada. I stayed put. My home became a haven for those leaving. I took in those who needed a landing place, supported by the gentiles in my community.

Although my people were being targeted, I did not feel moved to answer God's call or do His bidding to write the book He had requested. I did not answer the pull to receive new visions. Rather, the violence against Jews made me busy with urgent concerns, with helping families from Texas and Arizona get to Canada and Israel. They arrived in cars, minivans, and sport-utility vehicles crammed with everything from the Pesach china someone's bubbie 'brought from the old country' to canned food, camping gear, and in one case, a three-legged dog. The families slept anywhere they could, on floors and couches and the three blow-up beds that fit nicely into the library, sitting room, and main entrance hall. One group kept small fish in a bowl on the kitchen counter, and a turtle made a temporary home in the guest bath.

My nineteen-hundred-square-foot house slept as many as fourteen, and the local equine veterinarian made regular visits to the house to get all the animals their paperwork to cross into Canada. The Canadian Prime Minister put out the proverbial welcome mat. American Jews made their way across quietly, without fanfare. The violence, they believed, would be worse after the inauguration. They didn't wait, as their ancestors had in Europe. They moved while they had the chance.

I was furious. I wanted to be angry with God for letting this happen. Instead, I was simply angry. We had done this to ourselves by allowing greed and lies to prevail over kindness and community-mindedness. We had not revolted, rewriting the rules of the game. We had not as a nation radically changed our priorities, and that left us open to what I suspected could become an authoritarian regime. As I write that, I laugh at myself. Perhaps I am as politically naïve as my friends.

As feared, everything changed the morning after the inauguration, though no one imagined just how far-reaching the rollbacks on our freedoms would be. On that sunny, cold day, the President announced a 'new direction' for America.

"Effective immediately," he said, "the northern border will be closed. All immigration to Canada is halted. I am sending military troops to enforce this executive order." I gasped and looked at the live feed of the border crossing nearest my home. Sure enough, soldiers were already taking their place beside border patrol officers and the line of cars waiting at the border was turned back. "I am honoring my pledge to get the country out of the Paris Climate Agreement again. We do not stand by that egregious commitment. I am also ordering the immediate closure of the EPA, NOAA, Fish and Wildlife, and the Energy Department. With their closures, I am repealing all their regulatory rules and power." I turned off the television. There were more rollbacks, but it was too much for me to take in. I felt like I had fallen into an alternate universe.

Perhaps crisis is what I needed because I was suddenly galvanized. Courage overcame fear, and I knew that I would do whatever it took to stand up to the administration. This wasn't a matter of conservative vs. liberal. These weren't a few anti-Semites we could simply move away from. These were actions that would put the planet miles closer to the challenges God had foreshadowed. The step back was so severe I feared revolution, a civil war. I had already chosen a side. I couldn't silently allow us to skip down a path to our own demise. No matter how uncomfortable it would make me, I would use my talents as God had asked me to.

The instant I called upon God, He pulled me to Him. We met in our field. I sat down on the log. "I have to do it," was all I said.

"Are you sure?" God replied. He knew I was, but I could tell He wanted me to make a commitment.

I threw up my hands. "The government is making plans to auction off portions of the National Parks, and they're going to allow development in what is retained. I can already see the fast food restaurants popping up in front of El Capitan in Yosemite. They're going to cut down all of Calaveras Big Trees and sell the timber. There will be no more limits on fishing or hunting. The scientific information that was once available to the public on government websites has been scrubbed. This is beyond my comprehension. We no longer live in a democratic republic."

God said nothing.

"I don't know why this is the last straw, but it is. There comes a time when we must be courageous. Morality is not

68

relative. There is right and wrong. The need for action, to support the community, is greater than the possible personal negative outcomes for me," I said. "I was afraid of the consequences of acting when the price was smaller, when I might be ridiculed. But now the stakes are higher."

I sat for a moment collecting my thoughts. "I understand now about prophecy being not about being right, but about encouraging people to act. We have to change our course. I will be Your prophet and write this book, God, not only because I love You, but because I love mankind."

If it was possible for God to smile, He would have done so. I felt His presence warm before He returned me home.

****

The next day, I prepared myself for a journey. I fed and watered the cats, changed the linens on the bed, and ate a hearty breakfast. Then I sat on the bed in loose-fitting black cotton pajama bottoms and an old camo t-shirt. I was cross-legged, my eyes closed. My hair hung loosely about my face, tightly curled. It was a wet, rainy day. I pulled a green blanket around my shoulders. Closing my eyes, I entered a trance state and made my way toward God.

The trees in the orchard were mature and full of bright, ripe fruit. I couldn't quite place where I was, or why I had been called to this location, yet I knew it had to be important. Everything with God has meaning. Signs and portents are neither good nor bad. They simply are. The attribution of positive or negative has to do with whether or not we will get our way, whether we will feel lucky or disappointed. There are no mistakes and no unimportant details in a vision. There are no signs or symbols needing interpretation either. Messages in this world are direct, but you have to speak the language. I took in the particulars of my surroundings as I made my way toward God.

I spoke first. "Why, when I've been a seer the whole of my life, did You wait till now to ask me to write this book and receive these visions?"

God put what felt like a large hand on my shoulder, though in my sight there was nothing there but a shiny mist my eyes could barely perceive.

"Your earlier experiences were preparation for you, so that the experience of prophecy would not be jarring or unusual. This is the time because humankind is now at a critical juncture. The choices you collectively make in the next few years will set your course permanently. Earlier, and the message would have been lost. Later, and the information would come too late.

"I have given this same message to countless other people: the Dalai Lama, Thich Nhat Hanh, Desmond Tutu, Steve Irwin, Vandana Shiva, Wangari Maathai, David Attenborough, and Jane Goodall, but in different ways. Scientists have talked about climate change, mass extinctions, and overdependence on fossil fuels for decades. The clergy and sages have discussed living with compassion for centuries. Too few are listening. And those who seem to believe that most of My warnings are some sort of colossal conspiracy plot by business or the government or a stealth international oligarchy to ruin the lives of the working man, I do not even know what to say to that. So, I am trying My luck with you."

"I'll do my best to see and hear and write it all down exactly as I experience what You show me."

I felt God nod in approval. Then He became more serious. "What I am asking you to share with the world is important. As with the prophets of old, I need you to give a message of warning." I stared at God's brightness, my heart heavy as He continued, "Humankind's thinking is twisted. I am blamed for or hailed as the source of all things, good and evil. But that is incorrect. Humankind needs to know that you are co-creators of this world with Me, that the world's state is created from the cumulative effects of your collective actions. I am not the author of your lives. You all are collectively creating your reality.

"This world as you know it is ending, Elinor. The planet will go on, but human beings will not, not if you continue on the route of self-destruction that you have chosen. The great thinkers, scientists, theologians, and philosophers of your time have all said it, yet as a whole, you do not listen."

"How can my voice ring out above the din?" I asked. "I'm just an ordinary person, and one who a lot of people are going to think is crazy or posturing for attention."

"I picked you," God said, "because you struggle. I picked you because you are imperfect. I picked you because people can relate to you. If you can deal with the burdens in your life and change, anyone can. You have tremendous strength and passion that you cannot see in yourself, but those who know you can. And, most important, I picked you because, despite all that you have been through in your life, you still listen to and love Me. It is this last quality that I hope will move the hearts and minds of those who read your words. You are more precious and rare than you imagine. An ordinary person with an extraordinary, honest, and generous soul. You cannot deny who you are, Elinor. And I need you. I need your voice, your talent, and, most important, your example of courage."

****

God took my hand and began walking with me through the orchard. "Do you know where you are?" God asked. I nodded. I did. We had come to the orchard's edge. Inside the orchard's neat rows, peach trees were just trees, but here where the orchard ended, I knew our location. Ahead of us was a white double-wide trailer, my family home when I was a small girl. It was an impoverished-looking house, with rickety wooden steps leading up to the back door. There was no grass or landscaping on this side of the house, only a large expanse of sandy, hard-packed earth, where cars were sometimes parked. To the left of the house was the small orchard my mother called 'the family orchard.' In it were a dozen or so trees, most of which bore fruit. On the other side of the house, though I could not see it, was a sparse patch of grass and a large jacaranda tree. I knew the time when the house would have looked like this. It was a warm day in late September 1979. It was almost my seventh birthday. I had not been back to this house, even in dreams, since I was eleven years old.

"I brought you here because I want to show you the past the way I see it," God continued. His voice softened to a whisper. "I know you are frightened, and I know you would rather be anywhere but here, but I want you to share with others the depth of suffering that came to your father with the consequences of *his* actions. I want you to share not just the suffering that comes to the children of those who make poor choices, but to themselves too. I also want you to see your courage. I am going to take you into that house so that you will see what I see in you, a woman who went through unbearable suffering and can still cleave to Me. In My view, you are no different from Joseph, a boy who was a prisoner and a slave, but who became a man who soared because he listened to Me."

My eyes shifted toward the ground. I began quietly to cry. God seemed to be showing me my father's suffering as equal to or as important as my own. That hurt me. Where was God's compassion for the innocent?

God wiped the tears from my cheeks. "You have faults and make mistakes, My dear Elinor, but it is the purity of your love for and devotion to Me that captures My attention. You are so very brave."

I smiled weakly as God took my hand. Together, we walked toward the double-wide mobile home on the outskirts of the orchard.

****

The trailer looked just as I remembered it. The steps were still uneven. I recalled that once a frog had jumped out from under them at exactly the wrong moment and been crushed when the steps tilted then fell on its midsection, its guts forced out its mouth. I remembered too how no one but I seemed to notice and the frog stayed there for months, growing desiccated in the heat and the dust.

A fluffy, mostly white cat my mother had named Buckeye darted from beneath the house and dashed away. God

73

squeezed my hand. He seemed now to be both in front of and behind me, literally encapsulating me with His presence. I was protected. My vision was distorted by God's shimmer. I felt stronger, and also indescribably altered, there and not there, as if in a dream. I climbed the steps deliberately. As I did, the door in front of me opened. I crossed the threshold and found myself in the laundry room of my childhood home.

It was the smell I noticed first. My knees buckled, but I did not fall. The room smelled of hog manure, feed grain, dirt, and my father's sweat. I steadied myself. "You had to make us Jewish pig farmers?" I asked God. My tone was dry and disrespectful.

"That wasn't My decision," God whispered to me. "That's what I'm trying to show you. None of this was My choice. None of this is what I hoped or wanted for you."

God didn't need to tell me where He wanted me to go. I knew exactly what would transpire. God walked with me, through the pantry and kitchen, into the dining room and finally across the threshold of my parents' bedroom.

My father, a hulking man, lay on the bed. I, a girl of almost seven, was curled beside him, my head on his enormous belly. We were both watching television. It was a Saturday morning, and *Looney Tunes* cartoons were on. My mother and brother were away in town doing their bimonthly grocery run. My mom took my brother with her because he was small and my father wouldn't watch him adequately. I was older and more self-sufficient, and she left me at home so she had only one child to wrangle in the store.

My father looked young to me, perhaps because in this time warp, I was now older than he had been then. He wore only thin white boxer shorts, which was normal for him, if he wore anything at all. I was in my favorite nightgown, a red tie-dyed t-shirt that had been recycled from my father for a day camp art project. I recalled with a smile how the size disparity between me and my father had been so great that I had a hard time keeping the shirt on. If I didn't manage it just right, my slender frame would slip through the neck hole. But here that was no matter. I was lying down, curled into a tight ball next to him. My face rested on his bare stomach. I watched as my child-self smiled. I remembered how soothing it was to hear the gurgling sounds my father's guts made when he lay resting on the bed. It was a sort of white noise that relaxed me.

His hand was gently rubbing my head and neck. I saw on my childhood face a look of bliss. How I loved him! My father was everything to me. This enormous man with a bad temper, who embarrassed me by not wearing any clothes at home, was the center of my world. I remembered in my own heart how it felt to adore him.

"Please don't make me watch this," I whispered to God. I needed to be comforted. Leaning my head forward, I found God's chest. It was there, solid before me. God wrapped His arms around me, gently whispering, "Sh—" to me. He put one hand on my head, which released the tears in full force.

I didn't have to watch to know what was going to happen, so I turned away, but I felt it all again, standing there with God as silent witnesses to the events taking place in that room.

My father ran his hand down to the small of the back of my child-self. I stiffened because, in this experience, I felt everything he did to the little girl I once had been. It didn't feel right. It didn't feel gentle or loving. I was afraid.

Suddenly, he was on top of the child, a beast of a man, seven times her size. She struggled against him, but could not move. She was pinned down. He was too heavy, too big for her. Her lungs wouldn't work, couldn't expand with his weight on her. She wanted to scream, but nothing came out. She couldn't breathe and gasped for air. Without understanding what was going on, she felt a burst of dazzling white light and a pain so blinding that the last bit of breath left us both. She felt as if she was being ripped apart. She was passing out, darkness overtaking her. She could feel herself dying.

I went limp in God's arms, but He kept me from falling to the floor. Behind me, there was no sound save my father's grunting. I knew that the little girl me had split her soul from her body and was watching in detached disbelief from the jacaranda tree with Buckeye the cat.

The rape took only a short time, two minutes at most. When he was finished, my father got up and went into the bathroom. I turned around to see my child-self lying nearly lifeless on the bed. I felt the little girl's soul fly back inside, look at its own shell, and return, choosing life. I watched my child-self's confusion, and disgust at being dirty and feeling defiled. Bleeding and bewildered, she looked for her father, to be sure he was still in the bathroom. For the first time ever, she feared him. Then she ran away to the opposite end of the house, to lock herself in her bathroom and take a shower.

I sank to my knees and wailed in distress. How could he not have known that I loved him? How could a few moments that could not have been very pleasurable have been worth my life? Did he have any idea at all what he had done?

What surprised me is that I felt nothing for that little girl. I had no compassion or revulsion or love. I didn't wish she had fought harder or told anyone what had happened. I understood on a deep level that her response to what happened was the best she knew to do, but about her I felt no emotion. My therapists—I've had hundreds of hours of top-notch therapy over the years—told me that this lack of feeling is a normal response to trauma. Flat affect in reaction to horror is how some of us survive, but I felt ashamed by my lack of feeling. I believed that I should have felt more, should have wanted to protect or heal this child. I tried to push those judgments about myself aside and feel what I could in the moment.

God and I were alone in the room. Cartoons still played on the television. Daffy Duck was on the screen. I stood still and looked into God's face. He seemed more solid now, almost a cloud, almost with form. He wiped my tear-streaked cheeks. "Why didn't You stop it?" I asked quietly. I breathed in deeply. God had no smell.

"Because it wasn't My place," God said softly. "Your father made his choices. He made your world what it is. He took away so many things I wanted for you."

I thought about God not taking action. I could draw parallels between God and my father. It definitely felt like each used me in their own way. At least, God asked permission first. He didn't force His will on me the way my father did. But there was part of me that resented God's request that I serve as His prophet, sacrificing my goals for myself to do His bidding. I thought, too, about how much I loved my father. I had loved him mightily, even after this, even if he didn't reciprocate my feelings. Perhaps that's why I leaned so much on God. I wanted desperately to be loved.

I shivered with disgust. Even decades from that terrible day, I struggled with the consequences of that brief encounter and those that would follow over the next few years. The ripples continued to haunt me, playing out in ways that would blindside and often devastate me. There had been no boyfriends. No one had been interested enough to stay past my initial terror at their intentions. I'd had health problems from being abused so young. Though I begged them not to, the doctors took my uterus. It was dead and killing me, but I wanted so much to have a choice about children that I was OK with dying to keep the dream. How many men had declined even to meet me because I could not have children, could not build a family that would carry their genetic traits? And of course, there were thoughts of suicide, constant whispers in my mind that I would never be enough, that I wasn't of any value, that I was just a broken throwaway my father used, but did not love. All this wreckage was left by a man dead for more than twenty years. I wondered if he would ever truly be gone.

****

I looked down at my shoes and when I looked up, we were in a different place, a place filled not with horror, but with security and love. I dried my eyes on my sleeve. God was shimmering against the background of the lip of the forest. I sat down on our log and looked off into the distance, across the meadow, into the forest beyond. In my mind, this had always been, figuratively if not literally, the Garden of Eden.

God finally spoke, His words slow and measured. "I have, since the beginning of all things, given human beings the freedom to act as they choose."

My words were soft, an outward manifestation of the pain within. "How can You love me when my life has been this ugly? What of all the stories in the Torah where You smote this one and punished that one and parted seas and overcame armies? What of all of that? Why wasn't I worth helping?"

God snorted. "What of all that? It is true that I intervened in the past, but it never went well. I'll show you that later. No. Humans are the architects of your collective destiny. You are mature people, not like Adam and Eve who were no different spiritually from children."

"Do You not judge?" I asked.

"Not in the way you imagine," God replied. "You see, Elinor, I am both light and dark. In the beginning, as the story goes, I separated the darkness from the light. Yet, both are part of Me. Light is what you associate with good. It is not exactly like that, but I want to use terms you will understand. When people have near-death experiences, they often talk about the light that they see. This light is brighter, more radiant and vivid than anything you can imagine. That is what draws the souls that cultivate themselves through charity, good deeds, and a prayerful life. Light attracts light just as flame is drawn to flame.

"I am also darkness. There are souls that allow themselves to be consumed by darkness. When those lives end, their souls are absorbed into the darkness. It is the darkness of the plagues, a darkness that is almost tactile and utterly impenetrable. The light that those lost souls had still exists, but it cannot burn in the dark. Imagine being a light that cannot penetrate the dark. Would that not be a form of hell?"

"And what of punishment?" I asked.

"That is not something I require," God replied gently. "What good does it do Me to have a body or soul tortured for all eternity? I have no need to punish. Punishment comes as the natural result of your actions in life. Your father lost you, your love, and your respect. Do you remember when he called you at the university and you refused to talk to him? You put him on the phone with your classmates until he couldn't afford the call any longer. Was the loss of his only daughter not enough punishment? Would something more have helped you?"

"Yes. I wanted him to stop. I wanted You to send someone to stop him. If that couldn't happen, I prayed he would die, not when I was twenty-two, but when I was seven. When he did not die, I prayed that You would take me. He took my life, God! I've suffered immeasurably because of him. You know it's his abuse that damaged me, that prevented me from having children. You know it's my love for him that warped me, that made me feel so bad about myself that when I was a little girl, I started thinking about how I could kill myself. But You did nothing, so I stopped asking for Your help. I started to drink because I didn't have the courage to kill myself outright. If You had killed him, I would have been free. You didn't give me justice, and I deserved it."

"I would not do that, Elinor. Human beings are active agents in their lives. You each have been given the gifts of language and creative action. You have the blessing of consciousness. You have thoughts and goals and plans. You take actions to change the world around you. You make this reality. And you live with it, or do not. Your father used his creative capacity to hurt you. I will not intervene. And in the end, he lost as much as you did. I know you do not want to see this truth, but I want you genuinely and deeply to try to imagine a father who loses his daughter's love. What greater pain could he have experienced, Elinor, than to die knowing that you did not forgive him? I know this is no consolation to you, but he hurt too."

I was unconvinced. "And mercy? Where is mercy in all of this? Where was mercy for me?"

"Ah," God said. "What of mercy?" He paused. "Mercy is a most divine trait, one that I have given to each of you in the hope that you will share it with one another. Mercy, compassion, empathy, sacrifice; these are My greatest desires for you."

****

Suddenly, we were no longer on the log, but in the center of an African slum. I recognized it immediately as Kibera, Kenya. I studied in Kenya while at university and visited the slum as part of my fieldwork in international development. It was a heartbreaking experience to see poverty on that scale, affecting tens of thousands. It made an indelible mark on both my heart and my soul as a twenty-year-old student.

God and I stood on a winding path bustling with activity. Women waited at the spigot for an opportunity to fill a jerry can with potable water. Children ran from hut to hut playing chase games. A scraggly dog, covered in mange, yelped as a passerby kicked a stone at it. The day was hot. The stench was overwhelming. The air was thick with the smell of unclean

81

bodies, sewage, and decaying garbage. The sound, like the smell, was unrelenting. There were horns, crackling radios, shouting men, laughing children, hawkers and vendors crying out about their goods and services. It was in every way the slum I remembered.

God urged me forward. As I moved, I saw a young boy playing in the dirt. He looked about eight years old. God corrected me, letting me know without speaking that the boy was twelve, that malnutrition and hunger had stunted his growth. I watched the boy, following him as he rounded a corner to move deeper into the slum.

The boy and I both caught the scent at the same moment, turning our heads toward it. We smelled roasting meat. He ran in the direction of the alluring odor. I followed, with God behind. We ducked around huts made of metal scraps, wood, and plastic sheeting, away from the business area where we had started. There were fewer people here, and I felt less harried as we ran toward the source of the irresistible scent.

Finally, the boy stopped before a hut that was nothing more than a few bent sticks covered by a blue tarp. The door flap was open. Inside was an old man lying on a thin cardboard mat on the ground. He was terribly bony. His chest rattled as he took in a breath.

I turned and whispered to God, "He has TB." I had seen it before in Kenya. When it was this advanced, anyone could recognize it. I felt God nod confirmation.

Just outside the doorway of the hovel was a young woman. She held a small bird skewered on a stick. She was roasting it over the coals of her stove. The woman too looked sick. She was wearing a worn blue kikoi skirt and a once-white t-shirt so thin the light shone through it when she leaned forward. The skin on her withered legs was ashen and cracked. She was even gaunter than the man. Her eyes were hollow and jaundiced.

"AIDS?" I asked.

God nodded. "She will die soon," He said.

"And the old man within an hour or two at most," I said. Again, God nodded.

The boy stood outside the hut, eyeing the woman and the bird. He was clearly hungry. His tongue darted across his thick lips. The woman gave him a scowl, but did not move. She was exerting herself to cook the bird.

"Where did you get that?" the child asked in Kiswahili.

"I saw one of the dogs attack it. I pulled it away and finished it off," the woman said without emotion. She was squatting, almost sitting in the way Kenyan people often do, with their feet firmly planted on the ground and their buttocks nearly touching the dirt behind their heels. The old man rattled in the background. The woman did not move. She had given every bit of energy she had to wrest the bird from the dog.

Then a strange thing happened. God granted me the power to hear the boy's thoughts. He was considering whether or not he should steal the bird. Thievery was not normally part of his nature, but he was ravenous. He could see that the man was dying and the woman was weak. He knew that he could take the meat quickly because the man and woman would be unable to stop him. He struggled within himself, his hunger fighting with his respect for his elders.

"Mama," he said finally, deferentially, "will you share your meal with me?"

The meat smelled delicious. I imagined what a prize it must have seemed to the boy, the old man, and the woman.

But there was only enough food for one. The bird was as lean and as underfed as everything else in the slum, even the rats.

The woman looked at the meat and then at the old man. As she did, he began to cough. His cough was vigorous, wracking his body. The woman turned toward him. The thought jumped into the boy's mind that this was his chance. While the woman was distracted, he could take the meat and run. I wondered what he would do.

The moment passed and the woman turned back toward the boy. Their eyes met for an instant. She looked at the meat. It was well-cooked and juicy on the stick. She looked back at the old man. A dribble of bloody spittle emanated from the near side of his lips.

The woman stood, her joints cracking and popping. She was unsteady on her feet. She continued to look at the boy. Wordlessly, she reached forward, offering him the stick. The boy's eyes grew large. She nodded to him, her movement almost imperceptible. He did not wait for her to change her mind. The boy grabbed the treasure and darted off between the huts. "God bless you, Mama," was all that we heard as the boy disappeared.

The woman watched him go. She sighed, then fell back into the doorway of the hut. She braced herself as best she could against the doorframe, but she could not steady herself, and almost slithered down the support post to the ground. The old man rattled again, this time more urgently. She crawled to him, laying her head on his stomach, staring up into his face.

Now God let me hear her thoughts, too. She had wanted to give her dying father one final meal, one last gift, but it was too late for that. He could not eat and did not need to. She closed her eyes. 'We will die not long apart,' she thought, sighing with resignation.

God sent a gust of wind to close the tarp that was the tent's door, ending our voyeurism. Just before it fell, I saw the room fill with balls of light and the old man smile, opening his eyes to see his next journey begin.

****

Without a pause to discuss or even take in what I had just seen, God moved me to a new location. This, too, was a place I instantly recognized. It was the Kotel in Israel.

I stood in the courtyard near the women's section of the plaza. I knew it was Rosh Chodesh, the celebration of the new month, because I saw a group of women near the rear of the women's section in tallitot and tefillin, ritual items some view as reserved exclusively for use by men. Every Rosh Chodesh, a group known as Women of the Wall comes to the Kotel to pray. They pray as I do at my synagogue and in my home, wearing tallit and tefillin. They also read from the Torah, which was viewed by some of the gathered ultra-Orthodox men on the men's side of the plaza as an intolerable act.

On this day, there were about thirty women standing in the morning light singing joyfully to welcome the new month. They were an ordinary group of contemporary Jewish women, at least to American eyes. They were mostly older, in their mid-thirties and above, wearing kippot, tallitot, and tefillin, while singing loudly, joyfully, holding their siddurim. I saw what I would see at home in any Conservative synagogue; but this was not the United States. This was Israel, and the

Women of the Wall were, and still are, an outrageous and unacceptable sight to some ultra-Orthodox Jews.

On the other side of the mechitza—the fence that separates the genders—were three times as many men, a number of them watching the women with great intensity and resentment. While some were tourists, others had come specifically to confront the women for praying in a way they deem inappropriate. The angry men were cookie-cutter images of one another. They wore black hats, peyot, and for those who were old enough to grow them, long beards of nearly every color: red, black, brown, and grey. They were an army of aggrieved men who knew the 'right' way to pray. They would not let the women be.

When God and I arrived, the men were already making rude comments. Boys, not even bar mitzvah age, shouted slurs in Hebrew and Yiddish. They were egged on by older boys and men, men who if they had any real love for God would not have defiled their tongues with threats and jeers. Love evokes tolerance, not anger. I have never had any patience for those who do not allow others to pray in peace. To harass another in prayer is the true abomination.

It was then that the women's prayer leader brought out the Torah. It was a small Torah that someone had hidden in an oversized bag. The instant the men, who were standing on chairs, shaking their fists over the mechitza at the women, saw the Torah, two dozen or so literally looked to have lost their minds. Eyes filled with rage, they charged the mechitza, knocking down part of the barrier.

Immediately, the Israeli Defense Force soldiers who guard the Kotel jumped into action, trying to bring calm. Police officers also threw themselves between the charging men and the women. The women surrounded the one holding the Torah, trying to keep her safe. She held the Torah tight as one of the police officers attempted to pull it from her. Other women screamed when a barrage of items flew toward them: shoes, rocks, and bottles.

God and I remained in the plaza, watching the row. I couldn't help but cry. Those men attacking the women were not protecting our traditions and certainly were not protecting either the Torah or God. I could not understand how one Jew could condemn another for wanting to read from the Torah and rejoice in God's gifts to all of us.

****

The Kotel disappeared. I stood alone on a windswept plain. There was no vegetation anywhere, just a flat expanse of desert. The wind bellowed across the land, whipping my hair into my face, sand biting every bit of exposed skin. I tried to find a landmark to give me some indication of where I was, but found none.

"Where am I?" I shouted to God, knowing that He would hear me wherever He had gone.

When I received no immediate reply, I walked forward, hoping to find shelter.

After trudging up a slight grade for perhaps a mile, I came to a road. It was a two-lane asphalt track with nothing else visible in any direction, except sand dunes and an antique white porcelain bathtub abandoned on the roadside. In it sat God, His shimmer unmistakable. Atop His shimmer, where His head might have been, was a beat-up straw cowboy hat. I walked toward God. The wind died down as I did, becoming a comfortable, warm breeze. The day was mild. God rose as I approached.

"Really, God?" I teased. "You need a hat when You don't exactly have a head?"

God spun the hat into the air, where it vanished. "I thought it would amuse you."

I smiled. "It did." I paused for a moment, looking around, "Do you mind telling me where we are?"

"Kansas."

"Uh, no," I said. "Kansas is farmland: corn, wheat, soy, and sorghum for hundreds of miles. This is the Sahara or Central Australia or something."

"No, Elinor. This is Kansas."

God moved out of the bathtub. We started to walk together toward the west. The sun had passed its zenith and was beginning to touch the horizon in front of us. The wind was at our backs. Our pace was slow, leisurely. We had nowhere pressing to go.

"If this is Kansas, what happened?" I asked.

"Ah, that is why I brought you here," God said. "I hoped you would ask that very question."

I continued to walk, with God by my side, knowing that He would reveal to me what He wanted to in His own way and time.

"Everything that human beings created is crumbling," He said. I looked around. There was nothing to see but that single ribbon of asphalt, certainly no evidence of a once vibrant civilization. There were no more strip malls or pizza joints or mobile phone stores. No parks, schools, farms, rodeo grounds or theaters. There was nothing. What I saw around me was utter desolation.

God continued. "Elinor, believe Me when I say all civilization is gone, along with most of the plants and animals."

"The Christians were right," I said. "Armageddon."

"No, not like that," God replied sharply. "That theology assumes that I am the creator of your downfall. You did this to yourselves."

"Like my father spreading darkness, the woman in Kibera giving hope, and the fight at the Kotel creating discord and spreading intolerance. Perhaps this too is the result of our choices."

"Humankind is reaping what it has sown."

We walked in silence for some time before God continued, "People love to minimize the consequences of their actions, Elinor, even, or perhaps especially, those who act as brutally as your father or as abhorrently as those men at the Kotel. I hear it all the time in their thoughts, justifications that float to Me as tainted prayers. 'I only took a little bit.' 'They won't miss it.' 'I deserve it.' 'I want it.' 'Mine is the right way.' 'I am doing what You ordained.' 'They hurt me first.' 'They hurt my ancestors a century ago.' The excuses go on and on." God's voice was booming now. When He spoke like this, His voice began to lose its human-like qualities. I felt that this was the tip of what the prophets called God's anger. I cowered. The power in the sound that emanated from God made my head feel like a boil about to burst. God saw my discomfort and softened. "No matter what the action, there is a consequence to it. Life is not a zero-sum game. Even actions that seem benign have unintended outcomes. All of humanity bears those consequences, most of which are so subtle, humans will let yourselves off the hook for them. But is selfishness and incivility worth this?" God asked with a flourish, indicating the environment around us.

"When we say the *Unetaneh Tokef* prayer, aren't You listening?" I asked. "We pray, 'On Rosh Hashanah it is written, on Yom Kippur it is sealed.' That's what we're taught to believe, that all of this is on You."

"No, Elinor. Despite what you pray, that is not how it works. Yes, the Days of Awe are a time of reckoning, but only because it is you, human beings, who make your decisions about how you will act. You decide if you will eat healthy foods or stop smoking or involve yourself in charitable work or continue to underpay your employees or abuse your children. You write in the *Book of Life*, and you seal it yourselves."

"It doesn't have to be like this," I said. "That's why you took me to see the Kenyan boy," I spoke more quickly, excited by the possibility that what was being shown to me was not the only potential end. How might his life have been different if he had chosen to steal that meat? How might his character have changed if he had felt rewarded for stealing, if his belly had been filled by taking something from someone weaker? And how might his life change now because of that woman's generosity? "The woman sent out ripples. She got to end her life with an act of kindness to a stranger, love for her father, and the heartfelt blessing of a child. What better comforts could she have had in her last hours on Earth?"

I stopped to look at God. I no longer needed to be convinced that we, not God, are the engineers of our fate. I have never truly subscribed to the belief that human suffering comes from God's will. I also hadn't needed to be told that actions have consequences. I had lived through horrors and known others who lived through worse. I had experienced the way inhumane acts can break and warp a person. But would all those small acts really lead to the desolation I saw around me? I looked at the wasteland that had once helped feed a mighty and productive nation. "Are You suggesting that simple acts of kindness are all it will take to repair the world?"

God chuckled. "Not at all, Elinor. Acknowledging that actions have consequences is only the starting point for this journey we are taking. And this,"—as God spoke, a huge cyclone came out of nowhere in the distance, sucking in acres of dust as it passed by, disappearing into nothing as quickly as it came—"This is just the end result. This is where human selfishness, excess, and pride will lead. This is not the horror. This is the calm after the storm."

****

Chapter Four

שמע ישראל ה׳ אלהינו ה׳ אחד

Hear, Israel! The Lord is our God, the Lord is One.

– Shema

I lay on the cool grass of the golf course adjacent to my house, looking up at the sky. It was a dark night, and the heavens were an explosion of stars. I was alone, save the frogs that croaked incessantly from the pond. I listened carefully to the frogs, the richness of their chorus delighting me. On a recent visit to the Vancouver Aquarium, I had learned that half of all frog species will likely be extinct in 20 years, and all amphibians are threatened. I have paid more attention to the frogs since that visit, knowing that there would likely come a time, possibly in my lifetime, when all that came from the pond was silence.

It was an unseasonably warm night, and the moon was dim, so it was perfect for watching the meteor shower that was supposed to be at its fullest expression around 2 a.m. As I watched the shooting stars, I thought about my recent experiences with God. Could this really be the end for my species? Did a dinosaur ever cock his head toward a distant horizon thousands of years ago to watch a giant meteor hurtle toward Earth? Did he know the devastation that was about to be?

I rolled over onto my stomach and propped myself on my elbows, willing my eyes to see more clearly in the dark. Loneliness began to seep from my heart into my bones. My thoughts turned to myself and my future. If there were ever a major apocalypse or local war, I would not survive. I had always been fat and slow, and I would not knowingly harm another human being. It isn't who I am. If ever my circumstances called for me to kill or be killed, I would die. Perhaps that was part of why God chose me to see into the future. I had no horse in the race. I was being asked to see things that would not directly affect me, but upon which God hoped I might have an influence.

Despite knowing that my life is finite and that I would not last to see the worst of the outcomes of our actions, there was no question that I felt inexorably connected to everyone and everything. I was just one small part of something incomprehensibly enormous. I turned back over to look at the stars once more. Even before God asked me to chronicle my visions, I had started making plans to help my fellow man. I had seen the writing on the wall—literally—the writing on my Facebook feed. I knew that change had to come quickly, and our 'freedoms' were going to deteriorate fast. I started with what I knew best: knowledge and learning.

In my house, just behind me, was a great library. Over two decades, I had filled it with practical books on farming and gardening in my local area, canning and preserving, knitting and weaving, cultivating fruit trees in changing climates, and beekeeping, assuming that bees were not one of the first species to go in the mass extinction. I had books on acupuncture and finding local plants to use as herbal medicines. There were books, too, on philosophy and mysticism, folktales, and basic mechanics for survival situations. The garage was stocked with food and water, camping stoves, and gear for weather from below freezing to over one hundred degrees. I hoped that if a survivor of a one-day-to-come catastrophe happened into my home, they would find in it useful information and supplies that would help them rebuild community, if that was possible. Gazing into the heavens, I held out hope for radical human change, despite a concern that we had already passed the tipping point, and any hope of ecological recovery was lost. I had to lean into the faith God had in us. Pessimism might be my nature, but I would not give up so long as God still had hope.

****

I had only just finished writing down the last series of visions I'd had when it was time to commemorate the greatest of Jewish losses, the loss of our beloved Temple. The nation's political upheaval had left me frightened, exhausted, and pessimistic, the perfect mood of mourning for this particular holy day.

The better part of a year had passed since the last national election. Liberal groups were still in shock about the changes the regime had instituted. Changes to election law rammed through Congress gave the party in power absolute control over decision-making. The democratic republic was replaced by an authoritarian state. I had plans to leave soon. I could be smuggled across the border, but I would not go until the book was finished and handed off to my Australian publisher.

Friends had already found a home for the manuscript overseas. The Jewish Book Council in New York was closed. Books written by or about Jews were no longer being published in the USA. Because I had seen this coming, I'd sent the first chapters out with some of the refugees I'd helped before the inauguration. I could have gone to Australia at any point since the book was picked up, but I felt I had to stay in the USA at least for the short term. My fight was here.

I sat on the floor of the small sanctuary at our synagogue. Though it was dangerous, we met in defiance of those who would harm us. So far, our secluded synagogue and its members had avoided any violence.

It was Tisha b'Av, a sad day on which we fast, remembering the destruction of the Temples in Jerusalem and the beginning of our long diaspora. It is perhaps my favorite of all the Jewish holy days. I appreciate it because of the way in which it allows us to plumb our private sorrows in addition to our collective grief, in the hope of finding a way forward.

More personally, I relate to the idea of losing one's dreams, one's foundation for organizing life, and still finding the strength to go on. What does one do when the Temple, the very center of life around which everything else in the community is organized, is gone? What does one do when she knows that the entire future of the species is on the line, and her voice probably won't make a difference? What do we do when the state is seized by people who act with greed and hate? Do we rebel or succumb, and if we choose action, what actions will we choose? Is writing a book enough to set positive events in motion and create an opportunity to lead others to a brighter future? I had not yet defined the borders of my responsibility in God's effort to help human beings change. For the time being, I just took in the visions and wrote them down. I assumed more would be revealed.

The ark was covered with black cloth, as were the floors on which we sat. All the chairs had been removed from the sanctuary, except a few along the walls for the elderly or disabled. The room was dark. Each of us had only a small candle with which to read from the prayer book. The rabbi sang from *Lamentations*. His song was both beautiful and sad. I sat behind him and to his left, my eyes almost closed. Like him, I was dressed all in black, in older, shabby clothes, as if I were in mourning.

God wasted no time in continuing my visionary experiences. As the rabbi prayed, I rocked slowly back and forth, my midsection trembling wildly. That's my signal that God has a vision for me, a heating up of body temperature and shaking in the midsection. I asked God to take my spirit, but please to leave my body alone. I would have died of embarrassment to begin shaking violently or shouting out for God in an unknown-to-me ancient language, what academics call glossolalia, during the middle of the service. I still had some vanity that I was not ready to give up, despite God's assurances. There is a particular decorum to Jewish ritual, especially on this saddest of days. I did my best to hold myself in check, trying to force my interaction with God to come in some way that would not make me feel shame in front of my community.

When I could control the experience no more, I let my eyes roll back in my head. The lids shut loosely. I was no longer in the room participating in the Tisha b'Av ceremony. I was flying, not only in the air, but through space and time. The feeling was exhilarating, a freedom from all constraints.

Without warning, I was thrown hard to the ground. I stood up, dusting myself off. I was on an empty piece of hard-packed earth. I started. The smell of burning flesh made my stomach flip. The darkened land before me lit up as if a veil had been removed from a spotlight. I was blinded for a moment, until my eyes were able to adjust.

I was in a desert. In front of me was a statue of a man with the head of a bull, its arms outstretched before it, its mouth gaping wide. The overall impression was of ferocity, though I noticed its hands seemed small, disproportionate for its size. It was perhaps two stories high. The statue was bronze, hollow in the middle and open at the back, a type of ornate cook-stove or fireplace. I slipped from where I stood to the topmost part of a dune and hunkered down to watch.

From where I crouched before the beast, I could see that a fire glowed inside it, giving the impression that its abdomen burned a molten red-orange. From the fire came the stench of burning meat and hair. The glowing belly illuminated the monster's face in an unnatural way. The fire inside reached as far as the eyes, licking outward from the open orifices. Plumes of smoke billowed from its nostrils and mouth, suggesting that the idol was, in fact, alive. In the night, the monster looked as if it were both blinking and breathing. Even though I knew it was an idol, an inanimate thing, I waited breathlessly for it to move.

Around the statue were musicians playing flutes and drums. Others played tambourines and sang in festive jubilation. Men and women danced in a frenzied way, perhaps drunk on wine or intoxicated by the fervor of their actions. Sweat dripped from their arms and brows. Their light linen clothing clung to their wet bodies. Among them, in the center of the dancing, was a tall, slight man who seemed to be some kind of priest or holy man. He was naked save for a headdress of bull's horns and a sort of loose-fitting loincloth. He, too, danced, his eyes glistening with the intensity of his prayers.

The deep, exhilarating sound of rams' horns cut through the music. Three women were forced forward from somewhere I could not see. Each held a child less than a year old. The women wailed and pushed against the men who brought them through the dancing crowd toward the holy man. The revelers continued to dance. The presence of the women and children increased their fervor. The drums beat faster. The music became louder. The shofarot blew again. The revelry reached a fever pitch.

The ritual leader, mad-looking with his great set of horns, reached for the first of the children, snatching it from a young woman, whom I presumed to be its mother. She screamed as he took the baby. Uttering something I could not hear, he walked up a steep wooden walkway until he was level with the beast's mouth. He threw the infant into the fire. The dancers ululated as mother and child screamed in simultaneous anguish. The dancers were wild, indifferent to everything save their own celebration.

The fire crackled as more fuel was added to it from a platform almost hidden behind the idol. I smelled the oil, wood, and burning child.

I slid down the side of the sand dune in horror, because I realized these were Israelites. Bile rose in my throat. These people, my ancestors, were sacrificing children to this graven image. I had been face-to-face with Moloch, and I had to look away.

I closed my eyes tight, but the scene was seared into my memory. Though I tried to distance myself from it, I could not block out the event's sounds and smells. Sweat. Fire. Exultation. The burning flesh of innocents. The wailing of the child's mother. It revolted me. I felt nauseated. I prayed, "Please, God, let me move on."

****

The sounds of revelry ceased, and the sounds of battle burst upon me. I opened my eyes. I stood this time on a street in old Jerusalem. The city was under attack. Thin, terrified women and children ran in the streets. An old man fell not ten feet from me, struck by a short-bladed Roman sword. His sunken eyes clouded over almost before his last breath left him.

Ahead, I could see that the Temple was ablaze. Smoke curled from the beautiful structure as flames licked the sky. Small bands of young Israelite soldiers raced toward the fire, weapons at the ready. Roman soldiers pursued them. Civilians trying to leave the city were being cut down all around me. The streets were slick with blood, adding an acrid, iron smell to the smoke from the Temple blaze.

Bodies littered the alleys. Women screamed, doing their best to shield their children from their pursuers. It seemed as if the whole city was on the move, people racing in every direction, unable to see in the dark, smoke-filled air. The dread that the fire would engulf us was palpable. I watched the frightened civilians run, slipping on the blood-covered stones beneath their feet. I climbed atop an empty barrel, still upright beside a wall. From there, I watched the Temple burn, and I wept inconsolably for our God and our slaughtered people.

****

I came back to myself perhaps ten minutes before the Tisha b'Av service ended. I was only half-present. Part of me was still in the past, still watching the Temple burn, as we lamented its destruction in the present. I was lying on the ground, silently weeping, mouth open in a soundless scream. Like mine, most of the other congregants' candles had burned out. It was only the rabbi who had light, four candles, his own and three others that had been passed to him to allow him to read from the prayer book to continue singing *Lamentations*.

I sat up and pulled myself together, wiping the tears from my face with my sleeve. I did not listen to the words of the song anymore. I had just seen the Temple fall. The lament, as sadly poetic as it was, could not compare to that horrific experience. I didn't know how to respond to what I had witnessed. I was in shock and sat without thought or purpose.

As is customary when the Tisha b'Av service concludes, each of us went our separate ways in silence. I wanted to talk with the rabbi or one of my friends and tell them what I had seen. I wanted to follow the rabbi into his office, throw myself onto his leather couch and cry. I needed someone with whom I could share the horrors I had witnessed, but this was not the time or place. I stood in the hallway. My friends walked past. It would be months before I would tell anyone what I had seen, before I would have the opportunity to let anyone else share the burden of that vision.

Once home, I got immediately into the shower. I was overwhelmed by all I had observed and felt, as if the stench of the child sacrifice and scent of the battle had permeated my skin. I stuck the washcloth into my nostrils in an effort to get the stink out of me. Still in the shower, I began to pray. I demanded to see God, to know why He would show me something as terrible as that.

Out of the shower, I put on shorts and a tank top, my body pouring out heat and sweat as I prayed. I held nothing back, opening my mind, body, and spirit to God. I 'shuckled,' the Yiddish expression for swaying during prayer. When I could not raise my prayer high enough for me to reach an altered state of consciousness, I threw myself onto the floor, fully prostrate, frustrated, and exhausted, and begged God to come to me.

The instant my face touched the wood of my bedroom floor, I smelled the sweet grass of my forest meadow meeting place with God. I breathed in deeply, then raised myself from the damp earth. God waited for me on our log, at the line where forest and meadow come together. I walked toward Him purposefully, simultaneously wanting answers from Him and grateful that He would see me when I called.

"You cannot decide whether or not to be angry with Me," God said. There was sweetness in His voice, but also sternness.

"I am shocked and traumatized by the vision," I said.

"Fair enough," God replied. Though His mist did not change, I got the impression that He motioned for me to sit beside Him. I obliged. "You obviously want to talk about it," He added.

"Why would You make me see those horrors?" I blurted out the question. I did not censor myself, my revulsion at the scenes I had witnessed springing from my lips. "Those people, my people, they were throwing their children into Moloch's fiery mouth as a sacrifice. Didn't they hear their screams or their mothers' wailing? Didn't they remember Moses' pronouncement that this is not only a breach of our covenant with You, but also the most abhorrent of sacrifices? What could make them turn from You in that way, sacrificing children to an image that's only bronze and flame?" I gave God no opportunity to respond. "And the destruction of the Temple—Why would You force me to see that? The starving women and children. The old man. The screaming. The fire in the Temple. Did You think that what I imagined was not horrific enough? You needed me actually to be there?" I began to sob. I was not angry with God. I was overcome by what I had witnessed. The weight of the vision was too great to carry alone. If I could not talk with my rabbi or friends, then I would speak with God. I would talk with Him as I would have with them, without editing my feelings.

God wrapped what felt like an arm around me. The stench of the sacrificed children was stuck in my nose, the screams of their mothers ringing in my ears. Even though I'd washed it with coconut-scented shampoo, I imagined that my hair still smelled of the blood and smoke from Jerusalem. The memory of the Temple burning strengthened my sobs. I had never understood man's inhumanity to man. Yet, I could see many parallels with the present day. Even so, what I had witnessed in ancient Israel was more than my heart could stand.

God waved what I envisioned to be a hand over me. The scents, sounds, and sights abated. The vision began to feel more distant, like a once-painful memory that is now only a painted canvas. My tears stopped. I began to breathe normally. I sat upright and wiped the wetness and snot from my face. I could feel God smile. "Now are you able to discuss this?" God asked.

"Yes," I said. We sat for a few moments in silence. God didn't push me, always giving me the time and space to ask my own questions. Finally, I said timidly, "I don't understand why You showed me these visions. What is it that I am to know and share?"

"At Sinai," God said, "after the Exodus from Egypt, I spoke to the people." And there I was, at Sinai, arguably the most important event in the history of the Jewish people, for it was after the Exodus, at Sinai, that we became a community.

Sinai was less desolate than I'd imagined it. I thought I'd see sand dunes, like the vast desert of Egypt, but it was instead a sort of scrub desert with an occasional outcropping of plants and shrubby trees. The sky was clear, a welcoming blue. There was a breeze, too, that felt pleasing on my skin. I wrapped my arms around myself, rubbing my shoulders lightly. I felt in every way energized, electrically alive and at the same time completely at peace. I dug my toes into the sandy dirt at my feet.

I had been delivered into the heart of an enormous camp that stood in the shadow of a great mountain. Around me were the temporary shelters set up by thousands upon thousands of people. This was not the organized camp of the Bedouin, but the haphazard campsites of the itinerant and homeless. My moment of rapture over, I was quickly brought into the reality of the setting by the stink of improper sanitation and garbage that had been sitting in the sun. The people looked miserable and disoriented. The accumulation of campfire ashes indicated that they had been in this spot for several days. They were restless and seemed to want to move on. I could feel tension simmering in the camp. I wondered if what I was experiencing was the precursor to a riot. I prepared to run.

Not far in the distance, I saw that thousands of people had gathered. Those around me were moving in that direction. I walked with them toward the gathering, though I was still on edge. The group was larger than anything I had ever seen. Literally, there were masses of people in every direction, people who seemed, from where I stood, to be beyond number.

These people, too, were Israelites, like those I had seen sacrificing to Moloch, but they were not at all the same in a way I could not quite put my finger on. As ugly as the idea was, those who sacrificed to Moloch were agents of their destinies. They took action, misguided as it was, to create the lives they desired. The people at Sinai were broken in spirit. I recognized them, but I did not feel a kinship with them. They were timid and afraid, not realizing that they had more agency in their lives than they had ever had previously. Before this, they had been shepherded through every aspect of their lives. They were lost after being freed and looked with great fear toward the mountain.

But I had hope for them. They were clearly looking for direction. I believed they were on the precipice of something new and exciting.

Before us was a black pillar of smoke, a great column that reached far into the sky. It was impenetrable to human sight. It did not disperse, nor did it seem to come from any source. My heart opened wide. I recognized this column not by sight, but by feel. The column of smoke was no different from the essence I knew in the heat shimmer. This was the presence of God. I understood why the congregation was so frightened. Following an inexplicable emanation like this, being pulled away from everything they had known, was traumatic. They failed to see or experience what I latched onto so quickly. Inside this smoke was vastness, intelligence, consciousness, and compassion. It was a manifestation of Love. They had been brought to the desert by Love.

And then, from above the mountain, I heard a great booming voice. The sound made the earth shake and the wind cease. The tiny hairs on the back of my neck and tops of my arms stood on end. It was the voice God used that made me sick to my stomach and my head want to explode. Everyone around me dropped to their knees and covered their ears. Women screamed. Men groaned. The smoke pillar at the front of the gathering grew even darker, more intense, but the voice did not emanate from the pillar. It seemed to come from everywhere and nowhere at once. It was inside and outside my head, a heavy, heavy weight. I stood my ground, but closed my eyes against the noise. The tone God used was intense, guttural, and hard. I thought my ears might bleed.

"I am your God. I brought you out of Egypt to be your God. I have revealed Myself to you, all of you, to know Me as your God. You shall worship no other, through graven image, sacrifice, or prayer. I am your God, the only God of Israel."

The people screamed. Many fainted. Others shouted for Moses, begging him to make it stop. They prayed for mercy and for silence. Even I put my hands over my ears and asked

God to speak no more. Didn't God realize that no one could take in a message given in that way? It was too intense.

I had seen enough. I prayed to leave and was allowed to do so.

****

I was back at home in my bedroom, lying prostrate on the floor. When I got up, my body was heavy. I crawled into bed and pulled the bedcovers up around my shoulders. It had been a long and, in many ways, horrifying day. And yet, I was content. God had answered my question. I asked to know why I had to see these horrors, the human sacrifice, the loss of our beloved Temple, and I had been given the answer, along with the gift of witnessing our gathering at Sinai.

As I drifted off to sleep, I thought about all I had seen. In the Exodus, we knew little about making choices. We needed help, God's direct intervention because we could not help ourselves. We had accepted a mindset of powerlessness and could not lead ourselves out of that situation. We had to be given a set of rules to live by. With Moloch, we had tried to manipulate the world by manipulating a higher authority, giving sacrifices to ask a God to do our bidding. Doing so was a misunderstanding of how our relationship with the divine works. We needn't sacrifice our most precious gift, our children, to get the divine to act for us. We must act for ourselves. That's what God was trying to explain with the rules given to us at Sinai—how to act on our own behalf to create the best world for those to come.

Wasn't the result of the type of self-focused seeking from Moloch's worshippers the loss of the Temple? We were using our energy to try to manipulate God instead of creating the world we wanted for ourselves. I don't know that we could have defended ourselves against the Romans, but I do know that we were a people divided, a people rife with infighting and corruption during that period. We could have mounted a better defense if we had been thinking of our collective future instead of our individual or small group destinies. A more unified group acting together might have been able to create a different result.

Today, our situation—not just for Jews, but for all human beings—was no longer the same. We are no longer slaves who are told when to eat, when to work, and when to sleep, though there are forces attempting to press us into that position. We are powerful, creative individuals who are able to recognize that we've been given the opportunity to generate this world around us. It will be the best world possible if we keep certain principles first. It will be something less than that if we have different priorities. Most important, though, we have to look at ourselves not as individuals or as families, but as a collective group, united in purpose. If we want to see change, we need to be like the people of Israel who became united at Sinai. It's that kind of unanimity that is necessary to change the world. Then or now, unified action is required for success.

I wanted to be positive, but tired as I was from the day's experiences, I couldn't help but think that that level of cohesion is an impossibility in our contemporary, individualistic, polarized society.

My last thought before sleeping was of the *V'ahavta* and love. I came back always to whether or not we loved God as we claimed to, loved God enough to act with kindness toward our fellows. Love is a verb. It requires action. The Temple

107

was gone and the children sacrificed. We had already travelled far down a dangerous path, and yet with effort, I now believed there might be a chance to turn things around. We only had to make a decision. Change always starts with a decision, followed by effort. But did we have it in us? Too many of us, I feared, remained the cowed and frightened children of slaves instead of the proactive heroes in the best stories we tell each other. What kind of stories would we choose now to author in our lives?

****

Chapter Five

אלהים אלי אתה אשחרך צמאה לך נפשי כמה לך בשרי בארץ־ציה
ועיף בלי־מים

*God, You are my God. I search for You. My soul thirsts for
You. My body yearns for you as a parched and thirsty land
that has no water.*

– Psalm 63:2

It was bright and sunny outside when I woke up, but I felt
out of sorts. The previous day's anguish was still with me.
"Do the right thing," and "Be active, creative agents in the
world," were simple commands. Trite responses to the
difficult issues facing our species and planet don't take into
account the greed and, dare I say, evil inherent in human
nature. I was not confident that modest acts of selflessness or
community-mindedness could heal our complex problems.

I also remained resentful that God's role should be
passive. I didn't like the way God's stance smacked of, "You
made your bed, now lie in it." I understood free will, but I was
appalled that God allows blatant and horrific victimization.
Surely, if you see someone kick a dog, you intervene to
protect the dog. Wasn't that God's responsibility to us? Or
maybe that is my idealism. Not everyone protects the weak,

even God. The world doesn't work the way I want it to just because it's what I want. I was trying to receive God's message that it's humans who have to intervene for each other. Protection and support are our responsibility, not God's.

My black cat, Dov, jumped onto my chest and stared into my eyes, demanding as he did every morning that I get up immediately upon waking and fill his food bowl. I ignored him and continued to think. Judaism is based in part at least, on a belief in miracles. Creation was brought about by God retracting God's-self, what we call *tzimtzum*, so that the universe could come into being. Creation was only the beginning of a long string of miracles. There is God's intervention with Abraham, Lot, and Noah, directly shaping their lives and our history. There are the miracles of the Exodus: the ten plagues, pascal lamb, and splitting of the sea. There is the miracle of manna and Miriam's ability to bring water to the people wandering in the desert. All through the earliest parts of the Torah, our ancestors followed dreams and visions, signs and omens, to do exactly what it was that God wanted us to do. I couldn't help but think that we are followers of destiny, not creators of our own world.

Prophets have been a conduit between God and the people. Any of us could be a prophet, yet most people are too consumed with themselves to be able to hear God's voice. Prophets are those with an ability to move their own spirit aside to let God's words come through. God has chosen His prophets to give messages of warning, but over time, the work of the prophet has become misunderstood. Ask any Jew how to recognize a prophet, and you will get one consistent answer: the prophet's predictions come to pass. But that understanding conflates the work of a prophet with that of a fortune teller. A prophet's role is to give a message from God that God hopes will be heeded to abate negative outcomes. The prophet, like a parent, says, "If you don't stop misbehaving, a terrible consequence will occur." We tell children all the time, "Don't put your hand on the stove; you don't want to be burned." We do so in the hope that the child will not have to get burned to learn the lesson. We don't whoop at our great foresight when the child fails to listen and is injured.

Perhaps the greatest of the prophets was Jonah, because the people did take heed, and the terrible outcomes he predicted were thwarted because the people took action. If I had to be a prophet, I wanted to be like Jonah—a person who helped save others from the avoidable scourges of life. I didn't want to be the one at the end to say, "I told you so."

Dov began to meow plaintively. I sat up and continued to think about these inconsistencies while I followed him to the bathroom and his food dish. God does not always intercede. Sometimes, as they say, life happens. I do not like it that natural laws are not fair, that we could be wiped out by tidal waves or illnesses that had nothing to do with how good we are as people, how generous we are with others. But that God no longer dealt in miracles? That was harder to accept. What purpose then did God serve? Was He not to be our help in times of trouble? I could somehow accept the idea of God's inaction when it related to the deaths of 50 million people from Spanish flu and the anguish and devastation caused by 40 million lives shortened by HIV. But the deaths of *all* of us felt different. God could and I believed should do more than give a warning.

111

When I stood up from putting food into Dov's dish, I saw God sitting on the edge of the bathtub. I knew He was there to address my concerns. I said nothing.

"Part of loving Me, Elinor, part of having no other gods before Me, as you were taught at Sinai, is to act in the way I have taught you. Think not of a glorified version of the Golden Rule, but real community-minded action. That is the true meaning of *tikkun olam*, repair of the world. It is not your job to get Me to do what you want, but for you to be merciful and generous and act in ways that will uplift you all. This means thinking of the mitzvot not as good deeds, as many contemporary Jewish Americans do, but as real commandments, and to act in ways that repair the injury to the world done by others. To do that, nothing can come between you and Me. By this, I do not mean blind devotion, but rather concerted action to be in connection with your community and the world. Devotion to Me is attentiveness to kindness and generosity of spirit. Each time you make a choice that puts something between us, a decision that makes some object or being more important than your devotion to Me, by which I mean the active work of compassionate, just, creative community building, you will suffer consequences. These consequences come not out of My judgment or wrath, but as the direct result of selfishness and self-absorption."

A wave of nausea hit me along with bone-shattering pain. I moaned and fell to my knees. God made no movement to help me. Unable to stand, I crawled down the hallway from the bathroom to the bedroom and drew myself by sheer will onto the bed. Pulling the throw blanket tight around me, I began to sweat, although I felt very cold. My body shivered. I scooted myself up from the foot of the bed to the headboard, curling into a ball on the pillows. Another wave of nausea came. I looked around desperately for a container to vomit into. I knew I could not make it back to the bathroom. Every bone and muscle in my body ached in a way that made me feel my entire body was twisting up, contracting in on itself. "God, help me," I moaned. "Please."

God was no longer present, at least, not in any way I could perceive. I groaned, closing my eyes. When I reopened them, I found that I was no longer in my bedroom, but in my grandmother's house in Los Angeles. It was 1995. I was stretched out on a rickety travel cot in the back of my grandparents' home. The twin bed had a thin, worn mattress and a bar that caught me in the center of my sacrum when I slept. I no longer had my green fleece blanket, but the off-white twin guest blanket that I used as a bedspread. Cramps seized my stomach. The pain was so intense I began to cry.

A third wave of nausea rose from my stomach. This one, I could not hold back. I leaned over the right side of the bed and let the contents of my stomach go into the yellow bucket waiting there. I did my best to hold my hair back from my face as I retched, but it was no use. Small flecks of vomit found their way onto the ends.

I lay back, wiping my mouth crudely with my right arm. I panted, looking at the time-discolored popcorn ceiling above me. I could not move. My clothes were totally wet. I stank. I let the tears come silently, though they were no comfort for the pain.

God was with me now, crouching beside the bed. "Do you know what is happening to you?" He asked gently. The tone of His voice was the one we commonly use with the very old, very young, and deathly ill. "Do you know why you feel this way?"

I nodded slightly. I desperately wanted God to put a hand on my head and comfort me. Better yet, I wanted Him to remove this pain. God did neither. My tongue darted furtively across my dry lips in a futile attempt to wet them. I looked into God's crouching shimmer. My voice was hoarse from vomiting. "This is detox, alcohol detox, that I suffered more than two decades ago."

I closed my eyes. I imagined I felt God's hand on my chin. His thumb wiped away my tears and a smile graced His face as He lifted me from my suffering.

****

"That was dirty pool!" I shouted at God when I uncurled myself from the ball I had twisted into at the head of my bed. My finger trembled unsteadily when I pointed it at Him. I felt weak and ill. I had been transported back to my Los Angeles home, not to witness myself detoxing, but to experience it. "I went through that hell once before. I didn't need to go through it again." I stood. I stank of sweat and vomit and surprisingly, although I had not had a drink in more than twenty years, stale booze. "I didn't deserve that." I threw the stinking, wet blanket I had wrapped myself in on the floor and stormed off into the bathroom. I wanted a shower and was none too pleased to have God around at all at that moment. God stayed where I had left Him at the foot of the bed, saying nothing.

After I rinsed off the smell of vomit and brushed my teeth, I strode angrily and far more steadily back into my bedroom. In my closet, I put on clean pajamas. Even though I knew God knew what I looked like naked, I still had feelings of modesty and decorum. I rehung my towel in the bathroom and returned to sit at the foot of the bed with God. I wanted to tell Him off, but chose not to. If nothing else, re-experiencing the physical horror of alcohol detox would certainly solidify my sobriety. I noticed that the green throw blanket had been put in the laundry hamper. "Thanks for picking up after me," I said to God.

"You are welcome," God replied. Neither of us said anything for several minutes. Finally, God continued. "I apologize for upsetting you. I did not intend to traumatize you."

While I knew the latter was true, that God had not intended to traumatize me, and indeed, I did not feel traumatized so much as angry, I also knew that this was not a sincere apology. God isn't sorry for events in the same way that we are. I don't know that regret is part of God's experience. I saw myself for what I was, a tool that God had chosen to use. Surprisingly, I did not resent this. In fact, I appreciated that God was concerned enough about my feelings to apologize at all. I was, after all, only a mud puppet, a being that could be discarded and replaced without any repercussions to Him. And yet God expressed gentleness and mercy. I was moved and humbled. My feelings of love for God once again began to trump my anger.

I responded carefully, making an effort to defuse my rage. "After the election, I made a promise to You that I would write about whatever visions or experiences You asked. If that includes disclosing or reliving elements of my own life, even if they are difficult or painful for me to recount, I will live up to my word."

"Good," said God, "because I intend for you to freely discuss your addiction to alcohol. You, like King David before you, put a million and one things between yourself and Me. Doing so nearly killed you and could have harmed many others. How many times did you drive drunk? Whose health and welfare did you put in jeopardy by being loaded on the job? How much harm did you do to yourself through your drinking? That was all you being the creative agent of your life." I bowed my head. God was unquestionably right. I thought momentarily of the mess the nation and world were in. Most of us aren't evil. We're simply misguided.

God poked me with what felt like a finger, and I raised my head. It was time to go. We stood simultaneously and disappeared from my room.

****

God and I stood in my bubbie's tiny bathroom. A younger version of me was there, approximately eight years old.

When I was very young, younger even than this, I had dreamed of mainlining heroin. I had longed to feel absolutely nothing, an oblivion I knew the drug could provide. Call it a potential addict's intuition, but I had heard about heroin on the TV news, and it called to my soul. I hoped for opportunities to practice shooting up, so that I would be ready when the heroin I desired eventually came my way. A Girl Scout since the age of five, I believed in being prepared.

On this day, I had my first chance to practice being a junkie. The little girl me had locked herself in Bubbie's apartment bathroom. Bubbie was diabetic and took insulin injections daily. In the cramped room, the young girl I had

116

been squatted on the lid of the toilet. She was perched there with the synthetic pink fluff from the toilet lid cover poking between her little toes and the needle and syringe she had stolen from Bubbie's cabinet held delicately, reverently, in the fingers of her right hand. She tied herself off with a nylon belt and stuck the needle into the biggest vein she saw. Her goal was to draw blood. She knew that if she could pull blood from the vein, she could inject anything she wanted into it. She'd seen the veterinarian do it. But she did something wrong, and a huge, dark and purple-blue bruise immediately bloomed from the injection site at her elbow up to her shoulder and down to her wrist. Saddened by her failure, she removed the needle from her arm and rolled down her shirt sleeve. Throwing the rig in the garbage, she began to weep. After ten minutes or so, the child me dried her eyes and left the bathroom.

God and I remained in the bathroom, the overhead light still on. I shook my head. Then I saw my face in the medicine cabinet mirror. I looked grim. "What are you thinking?" God asked.

"I'm feeling heartbroken, thinking about how much pain that little girl was in, how she didn't know what to do to feel better. She had no one to turn to. She didn't believe her mother would stop her father from abusing her, and she was too ashamed to tell her grandparents anything. They loved her so much that she didn't want to upset them with her pain. Bubbie wailed whenever she saw my father hit me. I couldn't tell her what else he was doing."

"And what of Me?" God asked. "Why did you not turn to Me?"

117

"I did. You didn't answer," I said softly. "I used to pray, when my father was raping me, that You would end it. I prayed sometimes that You would kill one of us, me or him, it didn't matter. I hid in the closet sometimes, holding my breath in the hope that he would not find me. I prayed for Your intervention then, too. You didn't do anything. I had to deal with it on my own."

"Do you really believe that's true, that I ignored and abandoned you?" God asked.

"Yes."

"Then I know where to go next."

****

"Oh," I whispered quietly. This was not where I expected to come.

God and I stood at the foot of my childhood bed in the home my mother had moved my brother and me to when she left my father almost four years earlier. It was the canopy bed I had asked for when I was maybe five or six. The canopy had been destroyed before I was eight, as I had insisted on swinging on the bars that held and stretched the canopy's cloth. Now it was just a yellow four-poster twin bed pushed up against the wall of my bedroom.

I was fourteen. It was very late on a spring night, perhaps 12:30 or 1 a.m. My mother had met a new man and moved in with him immediately upon leaving her marriage to my father. They had purchased this place together. From the farm in California, she moved us to a smaller property in Oregon. Everything we had in Oregon was half what we'd had in

California. The property was half the acreage, and the single-wide mobile home was half the size.

Everything about the house was old and tired. The exterior edifice was rusted. The ceiling was yellow-brown from the previous owners' smoking. The carpets were crushed and in need of replacing. The single bathroom was hardly large enough to turn around in. To use the toilet, one had to rest against the washing machine. My room wasn't even a bedroom really, but an office off the kitchen. There was no privacy. In addition to the saloon doors that hung at the end farthest from the bed, the room had a three-foot tall by six-foot wide pass-through from the office to the kitchen. After months of my incessant complaining about lack of privacy, my stepfather had nailed a piece of plywood over the opening. It was an improvement over watching my mother peer at me as she did the dishes, but the rough-hewn board was a daily reminder of our poverty.

The one thing I liked about that room was that it ran the full breadth of the home, and at the end beside my bed was a bank of windows. During the day, I could watch the horses in the pasture. At night, I could see the stars.

Watching the scene, I extended my fingers, searching for God's support. He took my hand. I moved closer to Him, wanting to feel His proximity.

On this night, fourteen-year-old-me was not looking out the window, but lying in bed crying. I had never in all my young life felt as sad and alone as I did that night. My heart ached.

She was an unattractive young woman. Her hair was long, parted in the middle, and frizzy, without shape. Mom didn't have the money to have it professionally styled. The teen's skin was prone to breakouts. She was pale, puffy, and had recently gained a great deal of weight. When she had gone to high school the previous fall, boys had begun to notice her. She was ill-prepared for their attention. To discourage their advances, she began eating everything in sight. Her father and mother had both always told her that no man wants a fat woman. She took that information to heart. Her body had the bloated look of someone who had been eating only processed food for months. In addition to being sad, it was obvious that she was physically unwell.

Lying in bed, the fourteen-year-old me was wearing the same red tie-dyed t-shirt that had always been her favorite to sleep in, only now, at around two hundred pounds, there was no longer any danger of her slipping through the neck hole.

God and I watched as the girl rolled from her side to her back. The glint of tears on her face shone in the moonlight. She reached with her right hand toward the windowsill. There she retrieved a small, red Swiss Army Knife. She opened the largest blade and moved it into place. I could hear the delicate click of the safety lock from where I stood. The girl held the handle of the knife, watching the instrument gleam in the moonlight. She looked at it for only a moment. Then, with a determined expression, she plunged the blade into the flesh of her left arm and pulled toward the elbow. She winced in pain. The blade was far too dull for the job. She removed it to look at the incision. Though the wound bled reasonably heavily, it was little more than an inch long and had not damaged anything other than flesh. The teen shook her head with disgust, obviously upset that she had not been able to complete the task she had set for herself. She threw her right hand back, the bloody knife resting on her pillowcase. Her left hand fell to her side. She turned her face away from God and me to cry herself to sleep.

The moment she closed her eyes, the room filled with an incredible light. To say this light was brilliant does not do it justice. This light was not bright like the sun, but so dazzling that it illuminated every corner of the space. Seeing it, my soul expanded, as if I breathed from the very source of the universe. Rather than making me squint or look away, the vividness of this light drew me toward it, though God kept a hand on me to hold me where I stood.

As the room filled with light, it also filled with beings. They pressed into the space, expanding it. There were dozens of them, too many to fit naturally into the room. The girl opened her eyes. She was disoriented. Beside her crouched a figure who looked like a man. He was broadly built with deep brown eyes, wavy medium-brown hair, and a thick beard. He placed his right hand on her head and wiped the tears from her face with his left. She smiled and closed her eyes.

I watched as the angel ministered to her, taking her left arm and running his thumb over the wound. Behind him, the other angels looked on. I held God's hand tightly. God squeezed my hand. "This is only a memory," He said quietly.

"I know," I replied. Still, my heart expanded to see the vision before me.

Time moved to a strange beat that night. The girl awoke every hour on the hour. I watched her glance at the clock as she did. All the while the angels were there. She would smile into the face of the bearded one, the only one she could make out with her limited sight, then go back to sleep. He smiled at her, resting his right hand on her head and his left over her heart.

When morning came, the angels and light pressed together across the ceiling. The girl, the young me, looked at her arm. Though there was blood on the sheets, pillowcase, and knife, there was no longer any visible wound or scar on her flesh. She ran her finger gently over the place she had cut herself the night before, awestruck.

She got up and dressed for school. She could not look up toward the ceiling, though she wanted to. The power above her was not something upon which she could gaze directly. When she tried to look up, she had to turn away, feeling as if she might be blinded. Her face glowed with inner peace and gratitude. As she left the house, the light consolidated further into a ball ten feet or so above her head. It followed her the half-mile to her school bus stop, where she would finally watch it zip into the horizon.

God and I stood in the empty room looking at the unmade bed. "I don't want to talk about this just now," I whispered. My heart was full of conflicting emotions, from unconditional love to confusion. I didn't know how to feel or what to think. I realized that God had been with me in my darkest times. I had simply been unable to appreciate or feel the connection.

God was silent. The scene was gone.

****

God and I returned to my bedroom in the present day. "Are those the actions of a God who has no interest in you, of a God who does not listen to your prayers?" I shook my head slightly. "I am your comfort in all situations. I could not, would not, intervene against your father's choice to do what he did to you any more than I was willing to stop you from

122

drinking, but you were never, ever alone. I have always been with you to comfort and keep you.

"Elinor," God said gently, "what happened to you was your father's doing, not Mine. The world doesn't work the way you want it to no matter how much you hope, pray, or believe otherwise. There are rules I set in place that all human beings are to live by, rules I have chosen to respect as well. One of them has to do with allowing choice. This entire conversation is about just that. I made you in My 'image' by giving you the ability to create. You choose to use that power for good, or not."

I tried to listen as best I could as God spoke, but I was too sad really to care what He said. I slipped between the sheets of the bed, thinking about how it had felt to want to die and what it felt like, too, to finally have someone or something care that I continued living. God continued to talk, but it was only background noise.

"There was no one to rescue me," I whispered into my pillow.

I felt God move my hair from my brow, "No, there was not," God said gently. "There was not. And that is why I came. I am always present when there is no hope."

****

As soon as I was asleep, I began to dream. I was seated at a table behind a petite, blonde woman of about twenty-eight, who was dining with her husband and their infant. The child, in a pretty pink knit hat and matching blanket pulled up to her chin, was asleep in a stroller. The man and woman, obviously in love, stared into one another's faces as they dined. We were on a beach promenade; the smell of saltwater was strong on the breeze. It was a midsummer evening. I wasn't sure which beach we were on, because this was definitely not the United States. From the food, I guessed Europe, probably France, and I suspected this was the French Riviera. Over the water, a grand fireworks display had just ended. The man and woman laughed together, speaking softly as they drank wine and ate. The man thanked his wife for suggesting that they come out on this beautiful night. He had been tired earlier and wanted to stay in, but she had insisted that they experience everything they could on their vacation, and that included the fireworks display. They had not come over from 'dreary old England' to spend their nights cocooned in a hotel room. She wanted to drink in the sun and dance well into the night, the way Brits so often long to do when they enjoy beach holidays.

They didn't see the large, white-paneled truck hop the curb a few meters behind them. They were too busy laughing about how silly they would have been to stay in on a glorious evening like this. They didn't see the balls of light come hurtling down from the heavens, encircling each of them as the truck sped up through the throng of diners on the street, crashing into them, killing them instantly. The man and woman lay twisted in the street, the life gone from their eyes. All I could see of the child was the pink knit hat, covered in blood.

As the truck sped past, I noticed that with every dead-but-still-warm body on the street, there was a ball of light, an emissary sent to comfort the fallen and shepherd each soul to its next destination.

I awoke and recalled what God had said. "I am always there when there is no hope." I was comforted. Just as with the man dying of TB in Kenya, my early suicide attempt, and those whose lives were taken without notice by a terrorist, each of us was surrounded by the white light of Divinity.

****

A week passed before I heard from God again, and I have to admit that it was a relief. I needed time to process what I had seen and felt. I was coming to terms with the idea that God will not intervene, that He will love and support us, but that we are responsible for the path the world takes and the consequences that unfold. As soon as I had come to terms with those concepts, I had a new, even more disturbing dream.

In the dream, I sat in a sun-filled kitchen eating area, watching the news. I had watched the television reports for hours. All around the world, fish, dead and dying, were washing up on beaches. The oceans had gotten too warm for them. Of course, not every fish was dying. A handful of species could adapt to the warmer waters. However, the biggest problem was not the fish die-off, but the loss of phytoplankton, which are among those sea creatures unable to adapt to rising temperatures. They were dying off at such a rate that their extinction was imminent. These tiny sea plants that float freely through the upper layers of the oceans serve as the base of the oceanic food chain. With the phytoplankton virtually gone from the seas, the fish that relied on them for sustenance would starve, as would the creatures that fed on them. Thousands of species of fish, crustaceans, sea mammals, and birds were now dying. Scientists estimated that within a matter of weeks or perhaps months, the majority of the most recognizable sea creatures on Earth would be completely extinct in their natural habitats. The world would have lost all its whales, porpoises, dolphins, seals, penguins, otters, walruses, turtles, and sharks. All that would exist of these species would be those that were kept in global aquariums or zoos, but that was not enough to maintain viable breeding populations.

When fish die, they are usually eaten by other fish as they sink to the bottom of the sea. If their carcasses get to the seabed, they are eaten by scavengers and decomposers there. Nothing is wasted. But in this circumstance, God sent some of the dead and dying animals to the beaches, to be omens of man's impending downfall.

I found myself standing on Altona Beach, not far from Izzy and Amanda's home in the suburbs of Melbourne, Australia. Altona is a glistening white sand beach, a picturesque shore on Port Phillip Bay.

It was early morning and quite hot. On the cellphone I pulled from my right hip pocket, I saw Instagram posts from friends standing on other beaches, one in Venice, California, and another on Puget Sound. A college friend posted photos from a small island off the coast of Italy. A work associate did the same from a beach in the UK. Another friend sent word from Mumbai that India was affected. Still another reported piles of dead fish overwhelming beaches in Tanzania. A friend in Malaysia posted that the smell of dead fish was so repulsive that he had locked himself indoors with the air conditioner on full blast to minimize the smell and keep himself from vomiting.

On the news, there was no discussion of war or financial markets or celebrities making fools of themselves on drunken benders. Every pundit and talking head spoke of the unprecedented die-off of sea life. What would we do with all the dead fish? What would happen to the world's fisheries? What would the mass extinction of sea life mean for human beings? How would the people who rely on fish as their main source of protein survive? How would sushi lovers cope? Could the oceans be repopulated? Could anything at all be done to save the phytoplankton? The questions went on and on, and the scientific projections were gloomy.

Those not on the beaches to witness this cataclysm first-hand were gathered around radios and televisions to hear what was taking place. Even the Bedouins and Mongolians, those people who live farthest from the oceans and do not rely on fish in their diets much if at all, huddled around satellite internet connections and battery-operated radios to hear about the greatest, farthest-reaching natural disaster to befall humankind in the contemporary epoch.

The Australian government responded quickly to the catastrophe. The immediate fear was that millions of pounds of decomposing flesh would pose a significant public health hazard. So they deployed every vessel in their fleet: military ships, private fishing vessels, small yachts, even rowboats. Any boat able to run a dredge net was on the water working around the clock to scoop up the bodies of the fish before they washed up on beaches in Australia's most populated areas. There were no live fish at all in any of the nets. Not one. Once caught, the dead fish were taken to offloading sites in relatively unpopulated areas until the authorities figured out what to do with the bio-debris.

On the beach where I stood, the sand was thick with the bodies of tiny fish that the nets were unable to hold. These fish were so small that they were almost transparent. Sea birds

127

swarmed the beach, pulling these dead delicacies from the sand. I looked down to see a crab, maybe three-quarters of an inch in diameter, and I squatted so that I could get a better look at it. Its little pincers ripped apart the body of a fish. I sighed. I hoped that the little crab did not know that this feast would be one of its last, that soon there would be nothing at all for it to eat, and that it too would become carrion for the birds.

But that is not what drew me here. Standing up, I turned my attention from the boats on the horizon and the tiny crab at my feet. To my right, on this beach were the bodies of four enormous octopuses and squid. They were huge, bigger than a city bus. Three were already dead, but one, an octopus and the biggest of them all, was still alive. Even in the distance, I could see that it was at least two-thirds the size of my house. It was over two stories tall. The animal was dark, mottled slightly in sandy-earth tones. Its underside was lighter than its top, like a shark. You could see how it would have been able to hide in the depths, changing colors to match the sand or rocks, camouflaged light and dark as it floated or swam through open waters. I could not imagine how so large a creature could have found its way into this bay. I took its presence as an omen of terrible things to come.

The leviathan was feisty. As I drew closer, I saw that people had gathered, but were staying well back. There was blood on the sand and pieces of torn human bodies. Earlier in the morning, a pair of men ventured close, hoping to poke the creature with sticks and take videos to post on TikTok. The octopus had reached out and grabbed them. Horrified bystanders watched as the animal forced the men one at a time into its beak and ripped them to pieces.

I walked toward the creature, close, but not too close, and looked it directly in its eyes. I know it saw me. It was clearly an intelligent animal, a being I imagined understood life and death and knew that it would soon die. We had a moment of understanding. Of all the feelings I might have experienced, it was shame that consumed me as we looked at each other. It would die for our choices, and it knew it. There was anger in its eyes, condemnation as it looked at me. I clearly understood the message. "What you have caused cannot be undone."

****

When I awoke, I sat up against the headboard. God too was lying back against the headboard on the other side of the bed, flipping through the channels on the television. "Mind-numbing," He said, turning the machine off. I shook my head and smiled.

"Do you understand now, Elinor?" God asked. "Do you understand now the message that you must carry? If you lead a life that is just and community-minded, then not only will suffering diminish in the world, but you will fulfil the ancient prophesies and an era of peace unlike any you have ever known will be your reward."

I nodded. "That, God, assumes a level of unselfishness and grace that I doubt humankind has never known."

"Yes, it does. And I have not yet given up on you coming to understand these concepts, which is why we are having this conversation."

****

Chapter Six

קרא בגרון אל־תחשך כשופר הרם קולך והגד לעמי פשעם ולבית יעקב חטאתם

Cry full-throated, without restraint. Raise your voice like a ram's horn. Declare to My people their transgression, to the House of Jacob their failing.

– Isaiah 58:1

Still with my back to the headboard, I sat quietly. Slowly, I turned to my left to look at God. I half expected to see a tired old man, with a face lined from years of worry and frustration with people who rarely seemed to get it together collectively to live as God suggested. Rather, what I saw in that mist beside me was the embodiment of patience. God reminded me of the rabbi at my shul when a congregant or b'nai mitzvah has not adequately prepared the Hebrew they are reading or when someone giving announcements goes on too long. The rabbi just takes it in and lets any feelings he may have about it roll away. "God," I said, "You're not going to give up on us until every one of us has died."

"Correct."

"And You know that we will almost certainly all die, don't You?"

"Yes."

"And given what's happening in this country right now, You realize that we are moving farther from, not closer to, Your ideals. We are moving, often in Your name, closer to extinction."

"Yes."

I didn't know what else to say and so I said nothing. It was my turn to pick up the remote control. I flipped through the television menu for nearly three hundred channels and saw nothing of interest.

"Mind-numbing," God said again.

I turned the television off and looked at God. I understood well why few people believed the word of God's prophets, at least not while those prophets were alive. I also got why much of the world considered them, as someone in my Friday morning Jewish study group said, "sun-addled hippies who need to get jobs." Who in their right mind would believe that God talks to people so casually, hanging out and trying to find something worth watching on television?

I put the remote down. "I still don't understand why You can't intervene," I said softly.

"Sh—" God said, putting an arm around me. "There are two visions I want to show you. In one, I intervened. In another, I did not." God paused. "Are you prepared to see this now?"

"Yes. I want answers."

****

I stood alone on an uneven dirt road in a small village. It was cold out, though not winter. I felt as if I were on the set

131

of the film *Fiddler on the Roof.* The buildings in the town were wooden, and at most two stories tall. They were worn, the same wear I felt on the land. The place itself was tired from the long winter just past, but not yet bursting into spring.

To my left was one of the nicer buildings in this part of town, a two-story house with reasonably large windows with views the street from both floors. On the first floor, through glass panes, I could see men sitting in a dark room with equally dark wood furniture. They were Jewish men with great beards, black suits, and kashket-style hats. The man at the head of the table looked to be about eighty. From his features and clothing, as well as the scene, I guessed that I was in Russia or perhaps Ukraine in the early 1880s. The men were speaking with great animation, but when the old man spoke, everyone else became respectfully quiet. I could not tell for certain if the elderly man was the community's rabbi, but he was well respected whether he wore that mantle or not.

Upstairs the windows were covered with heavy curtains, but through one that was not completely closed, I could see the forms of women darting back and forth. I wondered if they were preparing for Shabbat. Their quick movements gave me the sense that a celebration would begin soon. I looked around for signs that might indicate the day or date, but found none. I deduced that this was the home of the most respected Jewish family in the village.

My contemplation about the people in the house was interrupted. I heard the sounds of a crowd coming down the road at a smart pace toward me. The group was made up of men of all ages, perhaps thirty in total. Most looked to be workers, but a few were better dressed, maybe merchants. At the front of the group were three men on horseback, each in uniform. The leader of the mob was a young, bearded man, an officer. He wore a fancy hat and tailored jacket. He rode a sixteen-hand black steed that pranced, animated by the group's agitation. The people walking behind the horses shouted and waved walking sticks, brooms, and farm implements.

I looked at the home to my left. I wanted to run inside and warn the people of the impending danger, but of course I knew that they could not see or hear me. Even if they could, I not only do not speak a word of Russian or Ukrainian, but wondered what the Orthodox men in the downstairs sitting room would make of me, a strange woman in pajama bottoms and a tank top. There was nothing I could do but watch the mob grow closer.

It took less than five minutes for the company to reach the building. Once there, they wasted no time rushing the door, making their way inside. Turmoil ensued. Chairs were overturned and smashed. The old man was wrenched from his seat and dragged into the street. The Jewish men rushed out after him, trying to pull him from the mob's clutches. The women upstairs were not attacked, though I could see their faces pressed against a slit between the curtains. Among them was an old woman, a woman I guessed to be the old man's wife. She looked out through eyes wide and moist with fear.

The old man was brought into the road and surrounded by the mob. They kicked and beat him until he could no longer stand. I stood in the center of the circle with him, facing him as he fell. The other Jewish men were being kept out of the circle by the crowd. They pushed forward desperately, trying to get to the old man, but could not reach him. They too were beaten and kicked, but it was the old man on whom the crowd focused its rage.

The young officer on the black horse shouted an order. At his command, everyone stopped moving. The other two riders dismounted and stepped forward obediently. The old Jewish man stood, doing his best to straighten himself, standing as tall as his aged spine would allow. His hands were relaxed, open at his sides. He did not give any attention to the open wound bleeding over his right eye or the swelling of his left eye and mouth. The man on the horse said something more, which sent the younger Jewish men into an uproar as they struggled with renewed strength against the hands that held them back from their teacher. The elderly woman upstairs screamed and was pulled from the window by two pairs of much younger hands.

The two uniformed men rushed forward, stripping the old man, tearing his clothes from him, so that he stood bare and cold in the street. He retained only his black leather shoes and worn black knit socks. The old man's skin was pale and sagging with age. Tears welled in my eyes and spilled down my cheeks. The Jewish men were shouting at the back of the group, still trying to get to the old man, who said something in not much more than a whisper that made them stop. Even if they had not heard him, they knew that he would not want them to endanger themselves for him.

The man on the black horse dismounted. He pulled a long baton from his saddle. Striding forward confidently, the young man flicked the elder's penis with the baton. The mob laughed at the circumcision. The old man closed his eyes. His countenance was one of complete peace. I had never in my life seen anyone look so regal in such humiliation. Then, I saw his lips begin to move almost imperceptibly. Though it was difficult to read them because of the swelling, it took me only a moment to know that he was no longer speaking the local language, but was saying the *Shema*. More tears came. I almost could not see the man's wrinkled face because of my crying.

Bored with his jokes about the old man's dangling member, the young officer remounted his horse. As he did, a melee ensued. The younger Jewish men would no longer be held back, and the scene turned into a full-blown riot. Only the old man and the young officer did not participate. The old man stood still, eyes closed in prayer while the young officer pulled out a pistol and shot him in the gut. The officer's intention was not to kill the elder man outright, but to make him suffer.

The elderly woman was again at the window. She screamed as the old man fell. The young officer turned his horse, forcing his way through the fighting mob. The old man, not yet dead, bled in the street, praying. I cried too hard to notice whether God sent any angels that day or not.

****

I next found myself in a small mud-brick home. In the main room, a large family sat huddled together. They had recently eaten a meal that included meat. The smell of the roast hung in the air. It was extremely dark. The room was lit only by a single oil lamp. A woman in the center of the space held two small children close to her. She watched the door intently, a fearful look on her face. Nearer the door, two men stood. In a back corner were three older people, two men and a woman, elderly but fit. The old woman fussed with the contents of a small basket that leaned against her left side.

I wanted to see what was going on outside. I could hear the wind howl through the cramped alleys. Though it was not a particularly cool night, I felt cold uneasiness wrap itself around my spine. As I went to open the door, God was beside me. "Stay inside!" He ordered. I did as I was told, noticing through the crack I had created that a doorpost was painted with blood. God shut the door tight.

"This is the night of the tenth plague!" I exclaimed.

"Yes," God said. "And you cannot be outside."

God and I sat on the floor in an empty corner through the long hours of that night. Eventually, the children nodded off, but all the adults remained awake. No one spoke. When the oil in the lamp burned out, we sat in darkness. The fear in this home, in the city, was palpable. I wondered—as the room's other inhabitants must have—if the night would be as interminable as it felt.

I guessed it was a little past midnight when the screams began. Each scream sounded amplified. There was no natural way to hear the screams coming from other quarters of the city, but we did. The sound was primal in its sadness. The wails came one at a time at first, then in dozens and hundreds. Everyone in the room held tightly to one another as the wailing and moaning—sounds so anguished they broke my heart—increased until we all pressed our hands over our ears, eyes closed in pain.

And then, suddenly, after more than an hour of screams and cries, silence.

The night dragged on. We listened, but heard nothing. Not a dog barking, a donkey braying, a sheep baaing, a goat bleating, or a cow lowing. Not one sound. Not cricket or frog or bird. The place was so preternaturally quiet that the hair on the back of my neck stood on end. Though the unnatural screams of man and beast had been horrifying, this silence brought even more terror to my heart. Even with God's presence beside me, I was afraid to give voice to my questions in that awful silence.

Then I heard the thud of men running in the street. It was past daybreak. I, and everyone else in the room, took in a deep breath. Men began banging on the doors. They yelled as they hit each door, "We leave now. Pharaoh's son is dead. We leave now. To the gathering place!"

The room erupted in activity. Everyone grabbed baskets and makeshift backpacks that had been filled with items of all sorts, but mostly food, blankets, and clothing. The men carried weapons, knives and whet stones, as well as staffs. Outside, two hens were quickly put into rough-woven bags for transport. A great flock of animals was already gathered about twenty yards ahead down the lane. There were also piles of valuables in the street—jewelry and fabric. I looked at one of the piles with confusion. "Loot," God said. "Some of the Jews have been looting the homes of Egyptians as preparations are made to leave."

"I thought the Torah said that the Egyptians gave these items up freely."

"Elinor, the Egyptians awoke in the night to dead family and animals all throughout their homes. They will give you the teeth from their very heads if you ask for them. They will give anything at all to get the Israelites to depart quickly. That is not giving freely. Now leave that for the people to take and go toward the place of meeting."

God and I left the family we had sheltered with, walking through winding, cramped streets. Egypt is a dusty place where everything except the palaces and monuments is the color of sand. The blandness of the palette added to the confusion of the departure.

There were already at least a half million people gathered, with animals as far as the eye could see. The assembly huddled close, as one might for a presidential inauguration or rock concert. I felt hot and uncomfortable. There was apprehension in the crowd and uncertainty, but also a sense of excitement. I felt the group's exhilaration at knowing that life was about to change radically, along with their fear of not knowing whether or not this change would be for the better. I turned to ask God a question, but He was no longer beside me. I was just one of the throng. However, because I knew the end of the story, perhaps I alone felt only a sense of jubilation.

Without fanfare, the group began to move forward. I imagined that somewhere ahead of us, maybe a mile, maybe two, maybe not that far, someone, Moses or Aaron, had given the order to walk. And so, we did. We pushed forward, people and animals moving in tight formation.

Our pace was slow, but we progressed. We walked through the narrow passages of the city into open country. The group spread out a bit, but not much. We all kept pace. The going was painfully slow, but I imagined that it was difficult to move this great a multitude of people and animals without causing a panic or stampede.

After three hours or so of walking among a group that—shall I politely say smelled like a barn—I looked up to the sky and asked, "Is it really necessary for me to do all this walking?"

God appeared next to me, this time as a very thin wisp of smoke. "Do you know how I know you are Jewish?" God asked, borrowing a line from a game I play with my friends sometimes in shul when I'm bored. I did not answer, as is the custom. God continued, "I know you are Jewish because even in the middle of the Exodus, while being graced with participating in what is perhaps the greatest event the Jewish people have ever experienced, even being given this gift, for which others would die, you complain about the walking!"

"I'm an overweight, middle-aged woman from the future who leads a sedentary life as a writer, God. What do You expect?" I smiled. God could not be angry with me, not for that. Besides, I had held back on the real complaining, which would come in about ten minutes if God didn't do something about my aching feet!

"And, God," I continued, leaning toward Him, "this group smells like a traveling 4-H fair."

If God had had a head to put in His hands, He probably would have done it then. I almost thought I heard Him think to Himself, 'And for this, I brought them out of Egypt,' but that could have been my imagination. I smiled sweetly at the hint of smoke at my side. "Please?" I asked.

And we were gone.

****

God and I sat on a muddy bank. I let out a great, "Ph!" the instant my butt hit the dirt. I almost immediately jumped up, afraid that there were crocodiles or clouds of mosquitoes waiting nearby to eat me whole or in bits.

139

If God had eyes, He'd have rolled them at me. "Did no one in your family teach you when it is appropriate to complain and when it is not?" God seemed a little exasperated with me. It did cross my mind that God was overseeing this whole Exodus and might have His hands full at the moment without babysitting me, but if that was the case, He should have picked a more physically fit mystic to tell His story.

"You could have sent horses," I said teasingly. "I ride quite well."

At this, God laughed. "You are completely irreverent!" He exclaimed. There was not a bit of malice in His voice. That God could appreciate my sense of humor made me smile.

Although I was physically exhausted, I felt only disbelief that I was on the march as part of the Exodus from Egypt. I was truly moved to be in this place at this time. To me, the Exodus was the greatest experience of the Jewish people. What could be more exhilarating to a person than witnessing her people being uplifted from slavery to freedom by the hand of God? I thought of how Alice pinched herself when entering Wonderland, to see if her experience was real.

I looked ahead, then flinched. I realized that I'd been so engrossed in my thoughts that I had failed to see the legion of angels standing in front of me with their backs turned. My eyes grew large as I took another step back. God stood and put a hand on my back to keep me from fleeing outright. Each angel was enormous, head and shoulders taller than any human. The angels had a distinct glow to them, a milky iridescence. Each held a shining sword in its right hand and a shield in its left. They wore heavy boots and cloaks that covered their shoulders, though I could almost make out what I thought were wings under the robes. I could not see their faces, for which I was grateful. These were not the caring orbs of light I had seen before. These were warriors, angels of death.

"Do not raise a sword to any of them, and they will leave you alone," God said wryly.

"No chance of that," I said, still staring wide-eyed at the angelic army before me.

Pharaoh's army approached with speed. The angels stiffened. God turned His attention from me toward the approaching dust cloud. I realized that in order for me to have a full view of events, God must have bestowed super-human vision upon me. After being startled by it for an instant, for the change in perception was great, I realized that the assembly of Israelites, six hundred thousand men and hundreds of thousands of women and children, along with millions of animals, was slowly making its way toward us. Behind them, the Egyptian army moved toward them at three times their speed. Even though I knew how the story ended, actually seeing the Egyptian army coming up fast on the fleeing Israelites brought a knot to my stomach.

A short burst of sound, at once a high-pitched screech and a low pulse, came from the pillar of smoke leading the mass of Israelites. The sound knocked me to the ground. I covered my ears. The angels responded by thrusting their swords sharply out to the right and flicking their wrists in what appeared to be a signal of readiness for battle. At the same time, two dozen or so angels from the far sides of the assembly flew off. When I stood up again, I saw that they had flown to the rear of the Israelite crowd. The whole group picked up its pace.

141

"This is a delicate operation," God said to me as He watched the Egyptians approach. "I need to get the Israelites to move a little faster without causing alarm and a charge."

"Even fear of the Egyptians won't get them to run if their legs hurt like mine did," I mumbled.

I felt God look at me, but He said nothing about my remark. "The angels will protect the stragglers."

As the Israelites drew near, the army of angels parted before them, forming the humans and animals into an orderly assemblage, much as a good shepherd and his dogs would do to a herd of sheep. The Israelites seemed unaware of them, but moved as the angels directed. Two men, whom I guessed were Moses and Aaron, led the group. They looked exhausted. Everyone did. They were dusty and their faces were smudged with dirt. Their lips were cracked and the skin on their hands was dry. As they reached the shore where God and I stood, just about everyone, man and beast alike, dropped to the ground, breathing hard.

Only the two leaders did not sit. They motioned with their arms, and a hundred young men came to them. I could hear nothing that was said, though I saw a great deal of gesticulation from the two leaders and a fair amount of head nodding from the young men. When the meeting was concluded, the young men, whom I assumed were messengers, raced back into the crowd to pass word of Moses' plan to cross the sea.

Night loomed. The sun dipped behind the horizon. Only a few rays glowed red-orange in the sky. The gigantic column of smoke that I had seen in my earlier vision of Sinai was present and moved swiftly from the front of the congregation, straight through the center of the people to the rear of the assemblage. The people pressed forward, sitting down as they reached the boundary set by those before them. There was no pushing or shoving. I could not tell what was being done to maintain order, but perhaps aided by the people's exhaustion, everyone was safe. As the last of the Israelites and their flocks reached the sea, the angels at the rear of the company formed a line behind the group. They were invisible to all the humans but me. The sight of the warrior angels would have induced panic. The assembled angels still had their eyes trained on the Egyptians, even as they assisted in keeping the Israelites together.

The people sensed the attention behind them and looked back. They saw dust being thrown up by the fast-moving Egyptian army and became frightened. Women screamed. A man shouted at Moses, "Were there not enough graves in Egypt that you brought us here to die?" Others said, "Perhaps if we turn back, surrender, we can live peaceably with the Egyptians again." Terror of what may happen once the Egyptians caught up to them swept through the group.

At the rear of the assembly, the column of smoke darkened. As all eyes gazed upon it, the wailing stopped. I could feel the divinity emanating from the smoke column. I almost expected the earth to tremble in awe. I fell forward, my head bowed. My heart raced and my body shook. I began to pray, whispering in a language I do not know, a language like Hebrew, but not. In my prayer, my love for God streamed out of me. I prostrated myself in the dirt, not caring about anything but expressing the gratitude I felt to be near and to know God.

No vision before this had ever been so thrilling to me. Although we are taught in Sunday school that the apex Jewish experience was to be at Sinai, because it was there that we became a people and were given Torah, I found being in the Exodus far more meaningful. At Sinai, we were already freed from slavery, and God showed Himself in a way that was too frightening for the people to accept. But at the Sea of Reeds, we did not know how God would save us. I could see Pharaoh leading the column of Egyptian troops. Exhausted and terrified, I knew that once the first person stepped onto the path Moses created, the people around me would put their trust in God—not the cloud of smoke that had led us—but the God they could not see who had exhorted them, through Moses, to leave Egypt.

I lifted my head from the dirt to see one of the angels standing over me. The angel said in a deep voice that was almost a growl, "You are to watch. No matter what you see or hear, watch and remember."

The angel's face shone so brightly I winced, wishing there was some way to turn down this extraordinary vision with which I had been blessed. The angel, though bright, was cold and not at all like the angels that had been at my bedside when I was a girl. This was a soldier without mercy. It had four dark eyes arranged in a square in the top center of its face, each with almost no white, and thin lips that covered a large, vicious-toothed mouth. The angel turned its back to me. It had removed its cloak. I could see several sets of folded wings. Then I stood, bowed, and backed carefully away.

I heard a voice in my mind. "Look away!" it exhorted. Reflexively, as if without the ability to disobey, all the Israelites did as the voice commanded—but not the angels or me. Once the people's faces turned and their eyes closed, the column of smoke, still clearly visible against the darkening night sky, flashed radiantly. It burned first red, then blue, then white. Again, I wanted to fall prostrate in prayer, but I did not. I had been commanded to watch, and watch I would.

The sight of the flaming column was magnificent, almost blinding. Actually, it was blinding to any person who had not been given supernatural vision, which was why the Israelites had been ordered to look away. I looked past the column of fire to the Egyptians beyond, realizing that they had been temporarily blinded by the light's brilliance. The army stopped just three miles from the Israelites. Their eyes, accustomed now to the light of the fire, could not adjust to see beyond it into the growing darkness.

"You are incredible!" I whispered aloud to God. I didn't mean it as a prayer, but as a statement of fact. The angel nearest me turned in my direction. I didn't need more than that to be struck quiet.

Past the pillar of fire, where the army had stopped, I saw that Pharaoh remained at the head of his troops. He spoke to men who looked to be his generals. I somehow could hear and understand their conversation. With the Israelites pinned against the water and the Egyptian army essentially blind, the leaders decided that they would rest their men and horses and attack in the morning. The order to camp was given to the Egyptian troops.

Immediately, as the order to camp was relayed to the charioteers, the great flaming pillar turned dark. Like a sentry, it stood at the rear of the Israelite column. Armed Israelite men of fighting age took up whatever arms they had and made their way to the rear of the assembly, to stand ready for an Egyptian attack.

The pillar itself was a manifestation of God and possessed great power, what men would consider magic. As it darkened, it sent darkness outward into the Egyptian camp, blocking the night sky and making it impossible for the soldiers to venture more than a foot from where they were without becoming completely lost.

In the Israelite camp, there was no darkness. Quite the opposite. As the Israelites peered at the sea, they were able to see clearly, under the light of a brilliant moon. The sea, which was no more than three or four feet deep when the first of the Israelites had reached it several hours earlier, was not so much a sea as a tidal floodplain. The water had already begun to recede with the tide before Moses lifted his arm toward it.

When Moses commanded the sea to part, a great easterly wind whipped across the land, pushing the water away from the Israelites and drying the land that had been beneath it. Within twenty minutes of Moses' command for the sea to withdraw, the combination of tidal movement and howling wind completely dried the area, allowing Moses to lead the first of the people and flocks forward through the reeds.

In the Egyptian camp, just as the supernatural fire and ensuing darkness had blinded the soldiers, the wind deafened them. The soldiers could hear nothing from the Israelite camp.

"Do not be concerned," I heard Pharaoh say. "They are pinned against the water and have nowhere to go."

But the Israelites did have somewhere to go, one path of escape. Their feet trampled the reeds, creating what was essentially an open road. All through the night, their way lit by the moon, the tide fully receded and the howling wind kept the land dry and solid beneath them. The Israelites crossed the sea. They moved as quickly as they could, pushing flocks before them and pulling wagons burdened with the cloth and gold they had taken from the Egyptians. The cattle, sheep, goats, and even a handful of camels kept pace with the people.

No one was left behind. The young and the elderly, who unaided would have been slow, were helped along. Some were even carried by angels. I walked across with the last of the Israelites, including a woman in labor and an old man in the process of dying, both cradled by warrior angels, who now looked human, carried as delicately as one would hold a fallen comrade or a newborn child.

As the last of the Israelites were in the center of the crossing, both the pillar of smoke and most of the angels moved carefully back toward the seashore. While they did this, the sun began to crest the horizon, lightening the sky. The tide returned. Water began to move quickly back across the road the Israelites had pounded down. I felt it wet my feet. Those still on the road hurried to finish the crossing. We started to run when the water reached our ankles. The wind died down just as the Egyptians found that they could once again see. They immediately began mounting their chariots.

Pharaoh, who had camped at the head of his column of troops, roared with anger when he saw that the Israelites were no longer trapped against the water before him. Enraged, he gave the order to charge. Hundreds of soldiers on single and double horse-drawn chariots raced toward the road still visible in the returning water.

There was only an inch or two of water on the road when Pharaoh began his crossing, yet the heavier chariots began to sink. Pharaoh's driver whipped the horses struggling to pull the chariot forward. With all their strength the horses pulled, and the chariot advanced, but only very slowly. By this time, all of the Israelites had completed the crossing. The pillar of smoke changed its dimensions. It became wide, a curtain between the Egyptians and the Israelites. Pharaoh roared and cursed, urging his horses and men on with word and whip. Lighter, single-horse carriages passed his own. Pharaoh howled with delight at this. He felt his army advancing and knew his chariot-borne archers would soon be within striking distance of the Israelites. His entire force was now on the sea road, pushing toward the Israelites, shrieking and shouting, as warriors often do on their way to battle.

The tide rolled in steadily. The water was now at least six inches deep. The horses strained against the mud, but the more they did, the more the wheels of the chariots sank into the seabed. Pharaoh raged as his chariot stuck for good in the muck beneath him. He and his driver jumped from the chariot and attempted to free the horses. Others did the same, but their feet and the hooves of their animals soon became mired in the mud. The soldiers and animals screamed in terror, trying to free themselves while water rushed in from the sea. They flailed and pulled, but water covered torsos and haunches. The water continued rising. Eventually, man and beast alike were drowned in a sea with a maximum depth of less than nine feet.

The Israelites stood on the far shore in stunned silence, watching their enemies drown. Then they spontaneously broke into song and celebration. The women took up tambourines, singing and dancing in jubilation.

I looked to God, who was again beside me. "This is a good day for Israel," I said.

"Their happiness will not last and comes at the expense of many lives," God replied.

"Yes, and they will complain all the way to Sinai, if the stories told in the Torah are true."

"They do not trust Me to meet their needs," God said. "As if I would bring them to safety only to let them die."

"Well, they had no experience to draw on other than this," I said.

"And drowning the Egyptian army was not enough?"

I was quiet. The question posed was one I could not answer. I thought about my request that God kill my father. He was dead now for decades, and it wasn't enough for me either. His death didn't end my pain. I imagined the Israelites felt similarly about the death of Pharoah and his soldiers.

After a moment, I said, "I'm tired, God. Will You return me home to rest before we discuss what You've shown me? This has been an incredible day."

Not a second later, I was in my own bed with the covers tucked carefully around my shoulders. God was gone. Ziva, my petite, elderly cat, looked up at me with disdain from where she lay. My return had clearly intruded upon a very important kitty dream. Since she was awake, however, I reached out, pulling her toward me. With Ziva tucked under my arm, I quickly fell asleep.

****

In my last dream, before I awoke in the morning, I found myself sitting on the log with God, waiting for Him to discuss with me the visions of the previous day. At last, He spoke. "You asked Me why I don't intervene, why I do not stop men from acting with evil intent or foolish men from causing accidents, or in other ways changing events to create a better world, if not a utopian society."

I thought for a moment, "I'm not sure I ever expected You would create a perfect world, but go on."

"Is that not what My intervention in human activities would imply? Is that not what you are praying for when you pray for the Moshiach to come? What is a miracle, but the upturning of natural order so that bad things would never happen to good people? Would My intervention in human activities not suggest a desire for Me to go well beyond ensuring that there is no war or injustice, but also that there is no more disease or hardship? When human beings pray for My intervention, are you not really doing more than saying, 'Help me,' but rather, 'Return us to the Garden where life is idyllic and easy?'"

I looked at my hands. They had begun to line with age. They are my mother's hands. I recall hers holding the steering wheel of her car when she was the age I am now. I thought about how we all grow, mature, and die and about how, during our lives, we each experience a variety of travails that become etched upon our faces and in the skin of our bodies—especially our hands. I looked up. God was right, only I didn't want to admit it.

God put what felt like a hand on my shoulder, leaning in to whisper in my ear as I stared at my hands, now folded in my lap. "Elinor, if you could perform miracles, would you?"

I pulled away from Him, horrified. "No," I said emphatically. God already knew this was true. I thought back to the first day I experienced myself as more than a visionary, the day I began to shake in awe and devotion. During that experience, I felt the power to heal sickness come to my hands, a great heat in my palms and fingers coupled with a confidence that I could remove disease from a person's body. I immediately flung the energy away, returning my hands to normal.

A little more than two years after that, in prayer, I encountered two beings. They offered to teach me magical words and powerful incantations that they told me I could use to ease human suffering in all manner of ways. I thanked them for the offer, but declined. I could not, would not, accept such 'gifts.' I wondered even then what the implications of such actions would be. If I brought rain here, did that mean I took it from somewhere else? If I healed a sick person, kept them from dying, would I then give that person the opportunity to do just as much ill as good? Wasn't there a natural order to things that included accidents and illnesses and droughts and other sorts of tragedies? If nature was an order that God created, how could I possibly believe I should wield the power to circumvent it?

God read my mind. "If all of that is true," he said, "then why is it you do not expect the same hesitations from Me?"

I said nothing because what God asked rang true. After a few seconds, God continued, "Elinor, I have intervened in human affairs in the past. I brought the Israelites, your ancestors, out of Egypt. I did this so that the entire world would know Me, know My commitment to humans. Humankind did not cleave to Me. They worshipped idols, or money, or power, or nothing at all. I made the covenant with Abraham and he with Me so that his descendants would follow Me. I chose you, the Jews, through that covenant, to serve as one example of a people who live in awe of and are devoted to Me. I encourage and uplift other groups in different, but similar ways.

"But the Israelites are a difficult group. In Egypt, knowing slavery and hardship, the people began to doubt Me. Even so, in keeping with my agreement with Abraham, I saved Israel in perhaps the grandest display of love and favor a tribe of human beings has ever known. I did it for love of humankind, to be near you. Yet even as I was saving Israel, they alternated between complaining and trembling with fear.

"When, along with the Egyptians, Israel experienced the first three plagues, they complained. The Israelites believed they should be spared. But how could they not experience these plagues? Was I to show myself as a force with incomplete power over the world? Then, when I visited the final plague upon the land, the death of the firstborn, though I exempted the Israelites from that scourge, they trembled in terror. On the march to the sea, the people moaned. *You* moaned. At the sea, believing that I had rescued them from Egypt only to abandon them to face Pharaoh's wrath alone, they begged to return to slavery. When they saw the sea part and heard the winds howl, they feared Me and mistrusted their ability to cross. Those who were unable to walk were carried. When safely on the other side, the people were not satisfied with their freedom. They needed to see Pharaoh's army drowned to know that they were secure. At Sinai, when I gave the entire people the gift of My speaking directly to each one, they fell to the ground in terror at the sound of My voice." God paused. "It is nothing but complaining, disbelief, and mistrust with humankind."

When I was certain God was done, I asked, "May I say something on behalf of the Jewish people, of all people?" I felt God nod His assent. "You have really high expectations of us." When I was not struck dead, I continued, "I'm not sure You realize how terrifying and awe-inspiring You are. I mean, You mostly hang out with sages, prophets, and angels, people and celestial beings who can handle being in Your presence. Normal people can't stand to be near You. Some might want to, but few can. If I can be honest, I don't really like to be near You unless You take a form like this one that I can understand and that isn't overwhelming for me. When You 'speak' the way You did at Sinai, well, God, if You wanted us to listen without falling to the ground, You should have given us different sorts of ears, because even though I'm accustomed to listening to You, I still felt like my head might explode when I heard Your voice. Imagine what hearing You is like for those who don't know what to expect.

"It's like the incident with the Golden Calf. The way I see it, You took a million or so spiritually immature individuals from a life of slavery, a life in which they had to make few significant decisions for themselves. Not all of them had great life skills, as we'd say nowadays. You had them endure three horrible plagues and watch seven more. You then took them from the only home and life they'd ever known; helped them narrowly escape their pursuers; and marched them across a desert where the only food they had to eat fell from the sky and rotted overnight. They lived in constant fear of want. When You got them to Sinai, You revealed too much of Yourself, scaring them to death. And as if that wasn't enough, You took the only guy who could interface with You, Moses, up the mountain, leaving the people to wait at the base. With all of that, are You going to tell me that You didn't expect the people to revert to what they knew from Egypt and make an idol to worship? They sought comfort the way they knew how. You might as well ask a frightened toddler not to hug a teddy bear."

"They lacked faith!" God half-shouted.

"They were spiritually immature!" I countered.

We were quiet for a moment. Then God went on. "Perhaps so, but do you understand why miracles and divine intervention are no longer the order of the day?"

Though I did not care to admit it, I did. I imagined God supernaturally repairing the environment. Doing so left us no room to change how we live, or stop the harm we choose to do to ourselves, others, and the world around us.

God spoke softly now, gently. "What kind of world would it be if I constantly intervened? You would be no better off than when you were slaves in Egypt because you would have no choice in how to live your lives."

I remained silent. I tried to imagine a world in which one could not do wrong, could not murder, rape, steal, or lie because God would intervene to stop it. I tried to imagine a world in which accidents and tsunamis and earthquakes and droughts did not happen. I tried to imagine what the world would really be like if there were no hardship at all.

As I thought about it, I realized that while I do not want to suffer, nor do I want difficulty for my friends, discomfort and tragedy are part of life. I could understand why Adam and Eve ate fruit from the 'tree of the knowledge of good and evil.' They wanted to grow up. Without the choice of facing calamity with faith and courage, how are we set apart from other animals? In a world with no trials or hardship, what meaning would there be in love, sacrifice, and generosity? How did those virtues play out when there was nothing negative to compare against? Yes, I continued to wish and was willing to work for a world in which there is less injustice, less inhumanity and violence, more ability of nations to meet the basic needs of their populations. However, the thought of living in the Garden, with no ability to grow or act with greater compassion—well, the idea made me envision humanity as a herd of fatted lambs, grazing contentedly in a field, not knowing or caring when the end would come. I knew instinctively that that was not the life for which we were created. My soul rebelled at the thought. It longed to grow, to be near God, and to act in ways that would be pleasing to Him and helpful to others.

"I intervened in the lives of the Israelites until the First Temple was built," God said. "After the First Temple was completed and the Israelites had been given direction on how to live, though I continued to speak to prophets and encourage men and women to live lives of devoted service to Me and one another, I have not overtly shaped global events. You are grown now. This world is yours to cultivate or destroy."

"What about the prayers we say like the *Mi Shebeirach*? Do You listen to our prayers for the sick and suffering, or are we simply wasting our breath?"

"Anytime you lift your voice and intention for another, I listen. The angels and I are with those for whom you pray and those for whom you do not. We bring them comfort in their illnesses and trials. The act of prayer is its own intercession, where you co-create with Me a more compassionate world. People will live or die. To be loved, comforted, and supported in that process, that is the true gift.

"But Elinor, tragedies happen. Children run into the street and are hit by cars despite having attentive, loving parents.

Illnesses occur and spread organically. These illnesses affect those who are depraved and hurtful just as often as those who are generous and loving. Accidents happen. In Texas, this month a homeless man lost control of a campfire. Eighteen homes were damaged or destroyed in the ensuing blaze. Whether the man was careless, mentally incompetent, or just distracted, the homes that were lost were lost because there was a fire, not because the homeowners deserved such a calamity."

I thought back to the time I spent in India in 1991. While traveling through Rajasthan, our group stopped at a roadside chai stand. I got off the bus and walked a few yards down the road. There sat two women, each with a large number of children surrounding her. They looked desperately poor. Before them, each woman had spread a gorgeous handmade tapestry approximately six feet by three feet in size. The tapestries were hand sewn in the Rajasthani folk style. It was clear that hundreds of hours had been used to stitch the appliqués and anchor the mirrors. One of the women looked at me. She asked if I spoke Hindi, which I did, a bit. She said, "Please buy it," indicating her tapestry. "It took me two months to make, and we have nothing to eat." Her children were covered in dust, pitiful to look at. One was obviously sick. Thick yellow-green mucus clogged his nose, and similarly colored discharge was in his eyes. Though I did not need the tapestry, I recognized its beauty. I purchased the piece for the equivalent of forty dollars in local currency. It was not enough to compensate for her work, but it was what I had. I literally gave her every rupee I had with me.

Decades later, I finally moved into my own home and had the piece framed. It hangs over my fireplace, the central piece of art in my house. Whenever I look at it, I wonder what became of that woman and her family. I feel a twinge of guilt and sadness that I did not have more money to give her at the time. Was it a good deed to give her every cent I could or a disservice to take the piece for less than its value? I will perhaps struggle with that question for the rest of my life.

The Rajasthani woman and her children did not deserve to live in abject poverty any more than I deserved what my father did to me. I understood in that moment that it wasn't God's place to set things right. It was ours. I thought of the Kenyan scene, in which the boy chose not to steal and the woman shared what she had. Sharing our resources, whatever they might be, was a start.

I thought, too, of the man I assumed to be a rabbi whom I had watched die. My eyes welled with tears as I felt a sense of pride in his courage. He did not deserve his end. I was inspired by this man. He knew his unjust death was near, yet he did not engage or argue with his abusers. His attention was intently upon his community and God. He died with dignity.

I was beginning to understand, beginning to put together the concepts God was laying out for me. However, I remained disturbed by the sheer breadth of tragedy that human behavior can create. We can wreak havoc of epic proportions, as happened in the vision of the leviathan, the octopus with the piercing eyes. My lips pursed. Humankind is responsible for an incomprehensible amount of harm.

Though I saw God's position more clearly now, I still had one issue on which to challenge Him. "And what of the Shoah, God? Did six million Jews, and the millions of others murdered with them, really need to die? If there was any time to intervene on behalf of Jews and other innocents, it was then."

"You are not the first to accuse me of inattentiveness in this regard, Elinor. But consider this: How many people had to act in collusion for those deaths to occur? Hitler could not kill six million Jews and millions of others without the complicity of millions. Millions. Thousands were active participants in the genocide. Millions turned a blind eye, not only to the Jews, but to all the others who died, too."

I started to say something, but God interrupted me before I could begin. "Let Me finish," God said sternly. "I want to put this in terms you will comprehend. It sickened Me to watch what happened in World War II," God said. "Language does not have enough adjectives to describe how disgusted, shocked, and appalled I was that humans would use extermination on the scale and with the efficiency the Nazis did. I spoke to humans endlessly, almost begging you individually and as groups to do what you could to intervene. Some did. Most did not. I collected the souls as they were dispatched. I would not intercede to save those people. That was and will ever be your responsibility as humans. You have learned to kill the 'other' as if they are of no consequence. When you destroy like that, kill the 'other' instead of seeing yourself in their humanity, you turn on yourselves.

"Do not think times or human actions are significantly different now than in the last century or centuries before. There are genocides occurring regularly that collectively you do not stop. How many people watched films about the Shoah, convicting those who stood idly by saying, 'How could they let that happen?' but themselves did nothing substantive to help those in Rwanda or Cambodia or Darfur or countless other killing fields? What is being done for Syria, Afghanistan, Iran, or Yemen? Europeans and North Americans still think they can allow proxy wars without consequence, but ongoing global terrorism is evidence that the world has not changed. In the U.S., systems exist that oppress and kill indigenous people, people of color, LGBTQ individuals, religious minorities, and so many marginalized others. As you have experienced, that situation is worsening, and very often being done in My name."

God was angry. He stopped speaking.

I thought about a white colleague of mine demonstrating in the Black Lives Matter movement. She was filmed putting her body in front of black leaders, using herself as a human shield when the police showed up at a protest. She knew she was less likely to be shot than the black protesters. I thought, too, of slaves forcibly taken from their homes and sold on the auction block, beaten when they showed any sign of pride or desire to run. Was that substantively different from present-day human trafficking? I thought of the women in Afghanistan left to the Taliban after the hasty U.S. retreat. The Armenian genocide. The growing women- and youth-led uprising in Iran. The myriad abuses against indigenous populations in North and South America, Australia, and other regions. I thought about the most recent pandemic, in which people in some countries had access to vaccines and supportive care that others for a long time did not. There's so much injustice in so many areas, and, as communities, we mostly stand by and watch.

When we hear about people being killed in the streets, how many of us are willing to do anything other than post on social media that we are outraged? I might have written a few letters as suggested by Amnesty International or donated to Doctors Without Borders, but not much more. How are we then any different today from seventy or seven hundred years ago?

"My vision for humankind has been clearly articulated," God said. "You are to love and support one another, be My hands and feet in the world. Yet overwhelmingly humans choose to throw My beautiful people into ovens. From where I sit, that says much more about humanity than it does about Me.

"The time has come for humankind to establish the communities in which you want your children to live, to stop fighting senseless ideological wars and get down to what I have desired from you since the beginning of creation—to honor Me with the work of your hands. You only have to start the work and do your best. It will be up to others to finish."

I stared at God. I wondered how thousands of years of interaction with human beings could leave Him so naïvely optimistic and absolutely out of touch with human nature. How could the Creator of the Universe believe that such a ground-shaking shift in human perception and action is even possible?

I also marveled at God, because despite our glaring character defects, despite His knowing that we would likely fail, He still believed in mankind enough to speak with such passion and to urge us all on toward better days. He is the Father who knows that among His children, great outcomes are possible, but also that the kids are spoiled and will make poor choices, demanding gifts and treats that they are not owed. And still, He guides with a steady hand, hoping that change will come.

****

Chapter Seven

הגיד לך אדם מה־טוב ומה־ה׳ דורש ממך כי אם־עשות משפט
ואהבת חסד והצנע לכת עם־אלהיך

*You have been told, humans, what is good and what God
requires of you. Only do justice, love mercy, and walk humbly
with God.*

– Micah 6:8

I sequestered myself in my house and dutifully wrote
down everything I had seen and experienced. Detailing the
visions was straightforward. I did my best to be a good
journalist and write them without embellishment, as I had
experienced them. The challenging part of the process at this
juncture was deciding how in the manuscript, I should deal
with my doubts.

Doubts I had in abundance. I doubted the whole project.
To what end would all this work come? Humankind needs a
radical change if we are going to keep from throwing
ourselves over the precipice. While I documented my
experience, I couldn't help but think of the climate change
deniers, particularly at the highest levels of government and
business, who are keeping the whole world from meaningful
action that could prevent the worst outcomes of climate

disaster. Already scientists are saying that we've passed a tipping point, and even with massive shifts in culture and action, it might be too late to stop the worst of a process that is sure to bring cataclysm to the planet's species. We're at this moment in the midst of the Holocene extinction, the sixth mass extinction to ravage the planet. Everything God is asking us to prevent is already coming to pass.

Then there are the droughts, heat, and fires. Every evening when I stopped writing for the day and watched the television news, I saw reports about the wildfires in California, Washington, Colorado, Texas, and throughout Canada. I have lived in the West almost all my life and have never seen fires like this. The drought in California is unprecedented, with farmers battling urban areas for the limited water resources that remain. In Western Washington state, where few people have air conditioning in their homes, the heat is unmatched in level and duration. What bothers me most is hearing the very wealthy, who live in some of California's most exclusive enclaves, talk about quietly leaving. They didn't sell their properties in California, but when water restrictions began to affect them, they simply picked up and went to Idaho, Colorado, Wyoming, or other playgrounds, where they could live and use resources as they wanted.

The average person doesn't have that luxury, can't just leave because they don't like water restrictions. Even where I live, where water remains abundant, we put ourselves on voluntary water restrictions to be better stewards of the available resources. We agree collectively that it is better to pull back use now than to be forced to cut back to almost nothing because we squandered what we had. There are still a few who disregard this voluntary action, but the pressure of neighbors brings almost all of them in line.

I feel the growing consequences of climate change in my daily life. My neighbors and friends in all parts of the world are experiencing these changes, just as I am. They face massive hurricanes, prolonged droughts, unrelenting snowstorms in winter, and unbearable heat in summer. In Washington state, people complained when the shellfish were contaminated so they couldn't be harvested, and fishing restrictions were implemented because fish populations crashed. In Alaska, there's concern that one important crab species may have suddenly become extinct due to rising water temperatures. *Extinct.* But collectively I don't see us making meaningful change. Perhaps we recycle when it's convenient or buy a hybrid car. But for the most part, we upload Pokémon Go and merrily and obliviously drive around town looking for a Pikachu instead of being actively engaged in the work of community building and ensuring that the climate on the planet and the complex ecosystems we depend upon to survive remain viable for humans.

I grew hopeless in those weeks. I began to believe that it was too late to make any meaningful change. Even in conjunction with the work of others, would a book make an impact? Al Gore, one of my favorite environmental change champions, had more than fifteen years earlier starred in a wonderful film, *An Inconvenient Truth*. He published a beautiful companion book with it. But had either the book or film made enough of a change to turn our communities around? Not so far. Is there hope? Greta Thunberg suggests there is because we can change our social, cultural, and economic norms in order to get the outcomes we want. We don't have to do what was always done. Many people are trying.

I had to trust God and those taking action, even if to me the efforts seemed too little, too late.

****

Summer was coming to an end when I saw God again. I was out in front of a neighbor's house, picking fresh blackberries. It was evening. I had waited until the sun had almost set before heading out, wanting to miss the heat of the day. I had picked nearly two gallons of berries, more than enough for me to freeze and pull out later in the winter. I was finishing up, leaving the remaining fruit for the rabbits, squirrels, and birds. They too deserved some of the harvest.

I was glad God had finally returned. I was anxious to move the project forward. The political situation for Jews in the U.S. was worsening, and it was only a matter of time before my community felt the brunt of the growing violence. Even so, we did not stop living our lives as we saw fit. We continued our volunteer work and honored our holy days together in community. We were defiant. I used that example to gird myself to do my part to help stop the worst effects of climate change.

As I juxtaposed God's warnings with the efforts I and others were making, I couldn't help but think we were in a losing battle. In the period since I had last communicated with God about this topic, the Arctic global seed bank had flooded and a major scientific study of climate change had to be scrapped—both as a result of climate change. Floods, landslides, drought, and disease were devastating the West.

The federal government did nothing to abate the problems and actively passed legislation that made climate change impacts worse. I knew from my visions that the coming winter would be dangerous. Perhaps God didn't mind lost causes, but I was no Don Quixote.

"God, may I ask You a question?" I asked, not looking up from my work.

"Certainly."

"I don't want to sound like the Israelites at Sinai or during the Exodus. I don't want to doubt You, but," I hesitated, "does any of this matter? People aren't going to change. They rarely do. Only after it's far too late do they cry out to You for help and mercy. How is this situation different from any other desperate time?"

God was quiet. I finished harvesting and started to walk back to the house without looking in God's direction. He said nothing and did not immediately follow me.

****

I washed the berries carefully and put them in individual servings in small reusable containers to freeze them. Living in the country, with access to produce and farms, I realized how little I needed from supermarkets. In the winter, I'd take out these bags of fruit and have them as treats, a bright taste of summer in the darkness that was to come. Two gallons was plenty for me. I'd already been gifted a jar of blackberry jam, more than enough to last me until next season. I'd also been given apple pies and applesauce, fresh pears to put up, and tomatoes that I could make into twenty family-sized servings of spaghetti sauce.

We were close to self-sufficient up here, and we shared. An apple or plum tree provided far more than any one person or small family would use, and so we gave away what we did not need. I had planted a fig tree because none of us had figs, and they would be good to trade for apples, which were available in abundance for the whole of the summer. Even with our trading and gifting, we still left plenty for the bears and rabbits and birds and everything else. It was, in a way, a sort of idyllic existence in the midst of a me-me-me culture.

But I knew that this was an anomaly. I had also lived in places where all food came from the market, and in some neighborhoods there were no markets, only fast-food joints. In times of trouble, like an earthquake, or if the power went down, there was no way to purchase anything because all transactions are now exclusively electronic. If the power outage lasted more than a few days, inevitably there were riots and looting.

Of course, there didn't have to be a natural disaster for there to be riots. Race, class, and gender biases, among others, cause their own problems. I remembered what it was like to live in Beverly Hills after the O.J. Simpson verdict. There were riots all over Los Angeles. The police for the city—because Beverly Hills is its own city, not part of Los Angeles, which surrounds it— were at the border to prevent the spreading violence from reaching us. There we sat, with our swimming pools and stockpiles of food and water, in relative safety, lamenting the fact that our maids and gardeners could not get to us. They were kept out with the riff-raff.

****

God called to me in a dream two days later. He pulled me to our meeting spot on the log at the edge of the forest. It was a warm day.

"Act justly and with compassion," God said to me. "That is the sum of My direction to man." He said it simply, without emotion.

I don't know why, but as God said this, I thought of the movie *Se7en,* the crime drama starring Morgan Freeman and Brad Pitt. In the movie, in which a serial killer uses the seven deadly sins as part of a killing spree, there is a scene that particularly sickened me. A man who sees a prostitute is 'forced' by the serial killer to don a ridiculous harness with a huge sharpened knife as the penis, and then fuck the prostitute to death. The man who did this was utterly devastated psychologically. Even with the best treatment available, there would be no recovery. His life could only end in a haze of addiction or suicide. He sat there after his act, sputtering and sobbing to the police about what he had done.

Of course, that story was fiction, but it reminded me of Maimonides and his teaching that there are circumstances in which, with a gun to our heads, we are to choose death. We must not worship a false god, commit an act of sexual transgression against another (essentially, rape), nor do we murder. Put a gun to my head or my mother's or my child's, and I am to die rather than commit these acts.

Why? Because there are acts that permanently and indelibly diminish the soul. There are times when it is better to die than to harm ourselves in ways from which there is no recovery.

"I understand," I said to God. "That I do understand."

****

Then we were in Indonesia shortly after the massive tsunami. I recognized it from the media coverage of the tsunami in 2004 that killed approximately 230,000 people in Indonesia, Thailand, and Sri Lanka. On this island, as far as the eye could see, there was only rubble. It looked like ramshackle kindling piles tossed about, but the 'kindling' sticks were poles and trees and large pieces of timber used in construction. And there was mud, mud everywhere, on everything. The smell was terrible. There must have been bodies of animals, people, and fish under the mud because the smell was of decay and decomposition. I put my hand over my nose and mouth to keep from throwing up.

I closed my eyes momentarily against the horror and, when I opened them, I found myself in a new place. I saw a man sitting behind a desk. He was dressed in slacks, a button-down shirt, and a tie. He must have been in a government office in Israel because there was an Israeli flag behind him. He was on the phone, speaking softly in English with a thick Israeli accent. His voice was deep, his tone distressed. I couldn't quite make out what he was saying before he hung up the phone.

He leaned back in his ergonomic chair and sighed. He looked like he belonged outside, in hiking boots and shorts, with a sun hat that shaded his neck, like the farmers wear in Israel to protect themselves from the unrelenting sun. His face was lined beyond his age from years in the sun. He was muscular and seemed like someone who was new to desk work. He sighed again.

Reaching forward across the desk, he pushed a button, summoning his assistant. It was only a moment before she walked into the office. She was tall and thin with luxurious, rich brunette curly hair. Her brown eyes shone against her olive skin. She had an electronic notepad in her right hand. She wore a simple grey pencil skirt and a long-sleeved white blouse, along with impossibly high heels, the kind that would have been the cause of my death if I'd tried to wear them. She stopped in front of the man's desk, awaiting direction.

"They don't want our help," he said in Hebrew. "Israeli aid would mean acknowledging us as a nation, recognizing us as a legitimate state."

"What will we do?" the young woman asked. Her boss never gave up easily.

"We will send aid anyway, with the Americans or international aid agencies. Food. Water. Medical supplies. Make sure everything sent is unmarked. We will help because that is what we do. Don't the sages say that the best way to give support is anonymously? I would like to do more, and we will do more where we can, in Sri Lanka and Thailand. Our planes land in Sri Lanka in two hours. For the others, we will give in any way they will accept. Filling the need is more important than being thanked for it. And perhaps tomorrow or next week, maybe they will change their minds."

****

I next found myself in what can only be described as an inferno. I stood beside a road in a forested area. The land was dry, the trees surrounded by underbrush killed off by the drought. The air was thick with dark black smoke. I could hardly breathe. The heat was off the charts, the fire driven by a hot, dry wind. Every breath in felt like inhaling live embers. More than anything, though, it was the smell that held my attention. Yes, there was the smell of burning wood and brush, but the heat too had a smell, and that is what made me the most frightened. The smell of the heat was the smell of doom.

On the roadway, cars and pickup trucks flew past. Their headlights were almost meaningless in the smoke, but the drivers pressed on at seventy miles an hour or more. They had to. The fire was moving toward me quickly, pushed by the winds. The cars were not full, as one might expect of people evacuating from a fire. I expected to see vehicles packed with everything that could be stuffed inside. But no, these people were fleeing. Inside some cars there were dogs and cats not in carriers. One car even had a grey parrot perched on the back seat. Children held onto blankets and stuffed toys, their faces pressed to the windows. Not one asked about videos or questioned arrival times. There was little if any conversation. On every face was a look of terror. The drivers' faces were pinched in concentration. They seemed to be trying to follow the fog line, where it could be seen. I was terrified for them all. It was not clear that any of them would make it out alive. One accident and the way out would be blocked for everyone. They all knew that, yet they fled at full speed, praying under their breath that they would make it.

****

I was transported to a new place then. It was far away from the fire, though the smoke could be seen in the distance. I found myself now at some sort of help-center for fire evacuees. There were volunteers from all over Canada and the United States. Some were handing out gift cards for food. A truck outfitted with washing machines had been set up to allow people to wash their clothes with free detergent and a laundry additive that is supposed to take smoke odor out of cloth. There were trucks offloading water and blankets. Most touching to me, there was an animal rescue service that was taking animals into their care. Many of the hotels in town would take families, but not their animals, especially not the horses, pigs, goats, cows, and chickens that were pouring out of trailers. Most of the evacuees had no food for their animals, even if the emergency shelters or hotels would have taken them. The rescue service provided food to those who could keep their animals and was taking the animals that needed refuge until those displaced by the fire could find somewhere more permanent than a hotel or shelter to go to. There was no fee for any of these services.

****

Back on the meadow log, I began to weep. It was clear that humankind has tremendous capacity to love, to live selflessly, to be community-minded. We did it all the time all over the world. We helped our enemies. We gave assistance to strangers. 'What was wrong with us,' I thought to myself, 'that we could not sustain this type of activity or do it on a larger scale?' Were we capable of selflessness and community-mindedness only during a catastrophe? Why couldn't we share more and in doing so live better? What would it take to shift the paradigm? Could it happen before it was too late?

****

Chapter Eight

ונתתי לכם לב חדש ורוח חדשה אתן בקרבכם והסרתי את־לב האבן
מבשרכם ונתתי לכם לב בשר

*And I will give you a new heart and put a new spirit into you.
I will remove the heart of stone from your body and give you
a heart of flesh.*

– Ezekiel 36:26

I looked at God. I felt God looking at me. As I stared at
the mist column beside me, I wondered how God saw the
world. I knew how God presented His views to me. I also
knew that this perception had been edited, created in such a
way that I would be able to understand it and was not in any
way a complete or holistic understanding of God's
worldview. Were human beings like small children to God,
given digestible bits of truth appropriate to our age and
development? Did God give us information in the form of
bright colors and interesting stories as we might to toddlers
who are just beginning to learn about the world? Or was
humankind not even that spiritually advanced? Perhaps we
were more like loving dogs to God, being told, "Good boy!"
when we enthusiastically retrieved a large stick that had been
thrown for our amusement.

I did not put these questions to God. Doing so seemed insolent. In the years I had been speaking with God, I had become deeply appreciative of the time and attention God gave me. I feel a bit like a favorite, pampered horse. After a hard day, I am groomed and patted, watered, and fed. My stall is kept clean, and I am allowed ample time to run in the fields, given treats and a blanket. When I come up lame or in some other way am injured, my attentive Master tends my wounds and cares for me. In return, and though I do not have to, for this Master loves me in good and bad times, I provide my loyal and dedicated service.

God had not yet spoken, though I had been back from my visions for at least twenty minutes. I could tell that what God wanted to say to me was going to be difficult for me to hear. I waited. "There are things that you must learn that you cannot learn from Me. These are lessons for you personally. You must learn truly what it means to be responsible for one another."

God's voice was gentle. Panic rose in my chest. I exhaled audibly.

"However, there is an angel—"

"An angel!" I exclaimed, interrupting God.

"An angel," God said delicately. "They are an angel unlike any you have ever seen before. I want you to learn from them."

I was in shock. I recalled the angels in Egypt. Angels are not all the loving cherubs of Valentine's Day or the balls of light that help the dying. Angels, like those in the Exodus, are also powerful beings that would not think twice about harming a person.

God laughed and put a hand on my shoulder. "Elinor," He said. "None of My angels is going to harm you."

I looked at God dubiously. "My father was not supposed to hurt me either," I said.

God put an arm around me, squeezed me gently, and was gone.

I sat alone on the log contemplating my fears about this soon-to-be-introduced angel before I too went back to the place from which I'd come.

****

The angel walked up to me casually while I sat at the counter of a café, eating a Napoleon pastry. There's a place here in town, owned by friends of mine, that makes them in the late summer with strawberries, blueberries, custard, and whipped cream. I find each bite to be well worth the thirty-minute drive to the restaurant and the hundreds of empty calories.

The lunch crowd had just thinned, but I didn't want a table. I preferred to enjoy my treat in front of the restaurant's huge glass window. I had perched myself atop a tall stool and was enjoying tiny bites of the dessert, savoring it. I had come from an appointment not far away and had nowhere else to be for the rest of the afternoon. Looking out the window, watching the cars pass on the busy street in front of the restaurant, I was content.

It was the angel's smell that I noticed first. They smelled not so much of fire as of heat. I know heat has no odor, and yet the scent was distinctly that of heat—dry, crisp heat—like the odor of the sensation of one's nose hair being dried out on a very hot day in the desert, like the heat in the fire I had witnessed. Perplexed, I looked to my left. One of the most handsome men I'd ever seen was leaning against the counter next to me, looking at me. They were giving me 'that' look, a look I don't usually get from men. The man was middle-aged, with longish brown hair and dark, penetrating eyes. They were hip and a little grungy looking. They reminded me of a movie star playing a devilish character: alluring, handsome, and dangerous. I stared at them. Though the feeling that came immediately to me was sexual attraction, something wasn't right. It wasn't only that the heat scent definitely emanated from them. There was something inexplicable about them that made me uneasy.

I reached cautiously for the telephone in my handbag. Pulling it out, I put it to my ear as if I were speaking into it. I looked away from the man. "Can anyone else see you?" I asked into the phone, not too loudly, but loudly enough that the being beside me could hear.

"No," was the response from my left. "You are the only one." Their voice was as beautiful as their body, rich and powerful. If it were not for the ineffable quality that unnerved me, I easily could have fallen in love.

I breathed a sigh of relief, applauding myself for thinking to pick up my telephone instead of talking into dead air. The thing I most hated about speaking with God and His emissaries was that they could not be seen by the average person. If I spoke to them directly, I looked like an insane woman talking to her invisible friends. I turned a bit more to the right, speaking again into the phone. "Are you the one I was told to wait for?"

"Yes, I am the one." They paused. "You would like to leave this place?" The words came out less as a question than a proposition.

My heart fluttered. I put my phone away, picked up my handbag, and hopped off the stool. Though half the pastry remained on the plate, I abandoned it.

My car was parked in front of the restaurant. I unlocked the door and got into the driver's seat. The man from the restaurant, without opening the passenger side door, was suddenly sitting beside me. I put on my seatbelt and backed the car from the curb. A heavy-set black man, armpits ringed with sweat, drove a derelict maroon Cadillac southbound on the street. He slammed on his brakes as my car began to move. He hit his turn indicator forcefully and grinned. One of his front teeth was silver. I waved at him. I could see gratitude for the parking space wash over his face. For some reason, this little interaction made me feel good. The angel beside me seemed oblivious. They stared straight ahead.

Once on the street, I made my way toward the freeway, toward home. I asked the angel, "Is there any place in particular you want to go?"

"Wherever you will be most comfortable." The angel's tone oozed sex. I shook my head slightly, quickly back and forth, as if a drop of water had gotten stuck in my ear. The angel's behavior made no sense. Why would an angel God sent behave in a manner that was overtly sexual?

I looked at the angel out of the corner of my eye. They acted with complete indifference toward me. Unlike God, who treated me with tenderness, the angel was emotionally detached. They interacted with me, it seemed, because they had a job to do. While God showed me genuine affection, the angel had the same expression as a stereotypical DMV employee. I was simply one more uninteresting task to deal with before a coffee break. Why then was I feeling such a strong sexual emanation from them?

"I would like to go home," I said.

"Then we will go to your home," the angel replied, still staring into the distance. I said nothing more, driving fast toward my house. Though beautiful, the angel was beginning to frighten me.

At my house, I went directly upstairs to my bedroom. It is the place I feel safest. It also seemed to be the room to which they were willing me. The angel followed silently behind me. They made no sound as they walked. The only sign of their presence was the distinct odor of heat, nothing more.

After putting my purse on the dresser, I climbed onto the bed. My cats, Ziva and Dov, who generally greet me at the bedroom door, were nowhere in sight. I sat with my back to the headboard, making a little wall around myself with pillows. I pulled a large pillow to my chest as protection and stared hard at the angel. Both cats, who had been in the bathroom, plunged under the bed. Finally, I asked, "What is it that you want?"

The angel flew toward me, hovering at nose level in front of me. They were overwhelmingly beautiful. I was enthralled, staring into their eyes, black pools with almost no white. I felt somewhat hypnotized. I closed my eyes. Despite their beauty and alluring presence, I did not like their stare.

I felt that they were no longer hovering before me and opened my eyes a tiny bit. They had gone into the corner. They stood quietly, watching me. Though they were wholly captivating, I could not get over the feeling that there was

179

something wrong about them. Part of me wanted to invite them into my bed, and part of me wanted to throw them out of the house entirely. "You are frightening me," I said, shaking myself from the trance they'd put me in.

"Am I?" the angel almost hissed. "I chose this form because I thought it would be pleasing to you."

"It's not your body, it's your presence," I said. The part of me that knew the angel was off won out. I was steeled. "Tell me whatever it is you need to tell me and go."

The angel dropped to the ground, now no longer a man, but a great snake. It hissed, pulling itself up so that its head and three feet of its great underside faced me. I gripped the pillow more tightly, but made no move. The angel lowered its serpent head, eyeing me once more. I was terrified. It was a great constrictor. I could feel it deciding whether or not to crush the life out of me. I looked toward heaven. I was certain this was not the angel I had been promised. "God," I cried. "This is not the angel You promised to send. Take it from my sight."

The snake let out a deep, guttural scream. It began to shrink in on itself, to contract to a central point that swallowed up both its form and mass. I watched in horror, but also relief. I had been captivated by the angel's preternatural beauty and the hypnotic stare they possessed. Not all beautiful things under the sun are kind.

The being was gone. I stared at where it had been on my bedroom floor. It left no mark. The only reminder of it was the smell of heat in the room. I got up and opened a window. It was an unseasonably hot day out. The wind blew. It was only moments before the smell dissipated entirely.

I lay back against the headboard again. The cats made their way gingerly out from under the bed. Dov put his front paws and head across my left knee. He had brought his favorite toy rat with him, and dropped it beside my thigh before he lay down on top of it. Ziva jumped onto the pillows and sprawled out, putting her head on my right shoulder. We all stared into the space where the entity had been. An hour went by. None of us moved.

As the immediacy of the danger passed, the cats purred. I started to nod off. The fear I had experienced, as well as the adrenaline rush, exhausted me. Try as I might to keep my eyes open, for there was still part of me that expected the being to return, I could not. It was not long before I was fast asleep.

****

Immediately, I began to dream. I stood atop a mountain in an arid highland range. The terrain was dry, a scrubland. There were no trees on this peak, just craggy outcroppings and sparse bushes.

Sitting not far off on a large boulder was a handsome young person, androgynous in their facial features, yet exuding power and virility. They wore a white robe, belted with a gold rope, and a white, calf-length cape over their broad shoulders. On their feet were brown leather sandals. Their hair was pulled back into a short ponytail. I knew instantly that they were an angel. They had the same heat-smell as the being I'd seen earlier in the day, and their eyes were not colored in any human tone, but flickered as if the irises were made of flame. The angel looked up at me, smiled, and rose. I watched them adjust the cape over what looked to be multiple sets of wings on their back. This angel engendered no fear or cautionary feelings in me. I watched them walk toward me. Their gait was regal.

"You are the one I have been waiting for," I said confidently, putting my hand out.

"I am Raziel," was the angel's response. They took my hand gently, awkwardly, as if unfamiliar with the custom. "I am the one who has been sent."

My exhaustion trumped my manners. I plopped down on ground, sitting cross-legged in the dirt. As I did so, I indicated that Raziel should sit beside me. Raziel looked around. Finding a flat rock to serve as a chair, they dusted it off before sitting. They were quite dignified.

"Do you know who it was that I met earlier?" I asked. I had the distinct feeling that this angel knew every event and thought, just as God did.

"Samael," they said.

"HaSatan?" I asked doubtfully. I didn't feel nearly important enough to receive a visit from the Accuser themself.

"Some call them by that title," Raziel said, "but it is important to name all beings correctly. That angel is known to God as Samael. Call them that. You have power over that which you can name."

I was quiet for a moment. Raziel was no nonsense. I did not want to aggravate them, but I also had a million questions to ask. "Why did Samael visit me?"

"To seduce you," Raziel said flatly. "It is Samael's job to seduce and accuse humankind. Their job is to confuse you, to pull you from the will of God, to fill your mind with want and desire such that you follow your basest impulses. It was Samael who planted the tree bearing forbidden fruit in the

Garden. It was Samael who seduced Eve into partaking of the fruit, into knowing that she has the same creative capacity as God. And it was Samael who seduced Eve into carnal relations. It was Samael who fathered Cain."

I hadn't expected that answer. My mind spun with another question, but I was too embarrassed to ask.

Raziel answered me despite my inability to speak the question aloud. "Samael took that form, as they said, because they believed that it would be pleasing for you. They allowed you to believe that they were sent by God to meet you. Samael placed themself in your path because God favors you with the gift of visions. Angels can lie, and surely Samael will and does, but we rarely have need. Humankind is far too willing to fall for lust, gluttony, and greed. We simply give you bits of truth or attention and let you do the harm to yourselves. We let you choose to act against your own interest. We give you choices. You learn no matter what you choose. Or you don't learn and try again. Humans have the choice to act in generous or creative or irresponsible or selfish ways, if that is what they desire. They have creative power. You, Elinor, call the results consequences. The Hindus call it karma.

"Samael," Raziel continued, "is the great snake, the consort of Lilith. Sexual relations are their most useful tool for trickery. It is easy to blind humankind with sexual urges. Samael would have taken you as a lover to distract you from God's work for you." I stared at Raziel, dumbfounded. Raziel seemed not to care about my surprise or the fact that their words disturbed me. "Samael knows that your greatest desire is for a partner. They would have given you that illusion, knowing that if the desires of your heart were yours, you would put your time and attention there instead of into the work God has given you."

"But Samael is neither man nor snake. How is it that they can take whatever form they like?" I asked.

"Angels have no gender or form, at least, nothing that you would understand. We are made of the substance of fire and wind. We are as breath, hot and airy, present but without mass. Recall the story of Moses and the burning bush. Angels are made of that type of fire, fire that emanates from nowhere and consumes nothing. We are the essence of fire, the essence of wind, not living or dead, but both at once. We are pure energy."

"Then why do you look like that sitting before me?"

"Because you are made of mud, of minerals and water with life breathed into you. You are a sentient being. You understand the world through your senses. If you cannot see or hear or touch or smell me, then I become a being of your imagination, a grand hallucination, and you will not listen. In a body, I make sense to you. And so, I conjured this body because it pleases you."

"And the wings?" I asked, pointing toward the cape.

"Because you expect them." Raziel paused. "Spiritual experiences take the form the person understands. A Jewish person sees Jewish symbols because those will make sense to them."

I nodded my head. "What of the angels I saw at the Exodus?"

"They are created for a different purpose than the archangels," Raziel replied. "They looked like ferocious warriors in part because they can be and in part because if they had needed to be revealed, they would have struck terror into the hearts of the Egyptians."

"And—"

"Enough." Raziel cut me off. Giving me a stern look, they raised their right hand, palm up toward me to silence me. I stopped speaking and bowed my head.

When they were certain that I would not interrupt, Raziel began asking me questions, directing the conversation. "How was it that Samael was unable to seduce you? They know human souls. They rarely miss when tempting one toward disobeying God's commands."

I looked at Raziel, forcing myself to overcome my reluctance to speak. "They smelled, um, hot," I whispered, looking at my hands. "I knew immediately that they were an angel, because of their odor, and, well," I said uneasily, "I just didn't trust them. There was something off about them."

Raziel grunted. I felt as if they were in some way disappointed with me, that I had not given a sufficiently articulate answer. I looked at my hands again, lying limp in my lap, waiting for Raziel to pick up the conversation. Eventually they said, "At least you are quickly able to recognize that which is not the will of God." Feeling like this was not a true compliment, I continued to look down.

My eyes brimmed with tears. I did not want to be a disappointment to Raziel or, more importantly, to God. Raziel reached forward, pulling my chin up so that my gaze met theirs. "It is no small accomplishment to know God's will. Most people cannot see it, though it is literally spelled out to every one of you mud beings." I stared into the pits of fire that were the center of Raziel's eyes. There was no emotion there, but there was approval. I smiled wanly, a gesture which the angel returned.

Raziel let my chin go. "I was sent here to teach you," they said, changing the subject. "I was able to appear because you rejected Samael." They paused. "Do you know what my name means?"

"No," I answered.

"Raziel means the Keeper of God's Secrets. I am the angel chosen to know what you would call magic, but what is in truth the secret of creation—science, art, consciousness, math, and intention all rolled up in one. God, as you were told in Torah, spoke the world into being. Although He did not have to, God chose language as the creative, binding force of the universe. He did this so that humankind would be gifted with the power to create with Him, through language, intention, and action. All three, in the right combination, are powerfully creative. In a different combination, they are destructive. Each human being chooses how to combine these forces hundreds of times each day.

"Every day, I stand in this place, atop Mount Horeb, and continue the creation process. While God's utterances have never ceased, I add to His words the creative power of the angels. I speak the magic that weaves the worlds together."

"What is it that God would have me learn from you?" I asked humbly.

"Anything you like. What is it that you want to know? How to heal? How to travel to the highest levels of heaven? How to cast spells to repel evil? How to divine the future? What is your desire?"

"I don't wish to know any of those things," I said. "I have neither the wisdom nor talent to be a miracle worker or a psychic. If God wishes healing for a person, there are other means through which He can bring healing, such as physicians. If He wishes that we know the future, He will tell us in a way that we can understand. If He wishes that I see the highest levels of heaven, He will take me there. If evil comes to me, I must deal with it. I want no special favors."

Raziel stared at me. I thought I saw disbelief in their expression. They did not speak, but studied my face for some time. I did not look away, though their gaze was intense and their thoughts inscrutable. Eventually Raziel said, "I understand why you were chosen. You have an unassuming heart." I said nothing. Raziel continued to look at me. After another long pause, they said, "God said that you would reject my offer to become a master of divination and sorcery."

"It's prohibited by the Torah," I said. "And, as I told you, I lack the wisdom to know who should live or die, who should be rich or poor, who should be blessed or who should suffer. Those aren't decisions I'm prepared to make. You said it yourself; I am just a being made of mud, with life breathed into me. Those miracles are for God to bestow as God chooses."

Raziel stood. The bushes all around the mountaintop burst into magnificent blue and white flame. Raziel smiled. They seemed amused. "Samael is angry. They wagered that you could be easily tempted by the promise of love or power. You succumb to neither."

"The love I want Samael cannot give me. What they offer is only an illusion," I said. "And power, well, when has the pursuit of power led anyone to anything other than a sticky end?"

The flames shot up higher as I spoke. I pretended not to notice, though I was scared.

Raziel laughed. Their laugh was like an audible twinkling of stars. "Samael is very displeased. You will meet them again before your days are through. But for now, you are under my guardianship, and you have much to learn. Let us go somewhere more amenable to the teaching."

****

I stood in a cabin on Puget Sound. It was early evening, but very dark out. A storm raged over the water, pelting the shoreline with sheets of rain. Lightning cracked and thunder bellowed. The cabin was only twenty yards or so from a thin strip of rocky shore. The floor-to-ceiling windows on the west side of the house jutted out toward the water. I was on the second floor. Even inside the house, I could smell the rain, sea, and forest. I breathed deeply. This place was my idea of heaven.

Raziel spoke. "Part of what is so exemplary about you is that you listen for God and do what God asks. Do you have any idea how rare that is, particularly in this age? Most people do not listen for God. They have not trained themselves to hear the divine words. They cannot hear God even when they try. Of the people who claim to be able to hear God and follow His plans, most are blindly following their own or their religious leaders' interpretation of scripture. A great deal of what they base their actions and beliefs on is not only untrue, but un-Godly. God has told you what His two main decrees are for humankind: first, that God is compassionate and so you are asked to act with compassion. While the world may be ruthless or indifferent, your capacity for creation allows you to create from a place of compassion. Second, live as God has commanded, with deference to and respect for all beings. The first command is self-explanatory. The second part I am here to teach you how to bring forth.

"The role of the visionary is to illuminate the divine vision of life. However, you may not speak the word of God if you are not prepared to follow God's precepts yourself."

"What does that mean?" I asked.

"It means leading an effort to create communities that are just. You are charged with helping build cultures in which people are not commodities, in which a person's value is not based on what they produce. You must help to overthrow the dominant culture, the idea that consumption is paramount. There are models throughout the world and from history that can be used. Each community can use its own template. For you, the place to start is with the people around you, the communities to which you belong. All cultures can be transformed to be more compassionate. Let the values of justice, equity, and compassion be your yardstick."

I had to be honest. "I don't know if I can live the way I would need to in order to be part of a transformation great enough to halt or reverse climate change and the sixth mass extinction. I'm not a survivalist or a minimalist. I'm accustomed to relative wealth and ease. I like having appliances and frequently eating out. I want sushi and meat and a car that's quite a bit larger than I need. I like books that I can hold in my hand even though I know that trees must be sacrificed for the paper. I want to continue to travel the globe to meet new people and experience different places and cultures. I like a little bit of decadence. How much of that am

189

I willing to change? Probably not as much as you will require. That's the truth of it."

Raziel looked at the ground, shaking their head. "Then I do not know that there is any hope." Thunder boomed behind me. I turned toward it. When I turned back to the window, I realized that I was alone.

****

The room in which I stood was outfitted with two overstuffed leather club chairs facing the floor-to-ceiling windows and a grand stone fireplace. I lit the fire before plopping down in one of the chairs. Pulling a throw from an ottoman, I curled into the chair with my feet under me. I put my head onto the corner of the chair while I looked at the fire and the darkness beyond. I felt like a total failure. I hadn't meant to displease Raziel. I wasn't even really certain how I had upset them so much that they would leave. How could I be blamed for being honest?

"Well," I said to myself as I brought my knees in tighter toward my torso, "you've managed to chase off Raziel in less than an hour. I'll bet that's some sort of record."

"Actually, it is not," said God.

I sat up. I could not see God's form in the dark, but His voice seemed to emanate from the other club chair in front of the fire. "God!" I exclaimed.

"Yes, I am here," God said.

I jumped up from where I was, practically leaping to the other chair. I sank into it, then got up, demanding, "Give Yourself form so I can hug You!" Leaning forward, I felt the form of a man and hugged it, whispering where I believed an ear might have been, "I'm so glad You're here."

I returned to my chair, and God laughed. "Raziel told Samael that they are losing their touch, and Samael told Raziel that they can have you because they have better prospects elsewhere. Samael says that they can turn you, but it is too much effort."

"In other words, I'm the latest gossip over the angel water cooler," I said.

"Something like that," God replied. He paused. "Raziel will return. I have told them that you will make an effort, Elinor. Try to keep in mind that they are not accustomed to hearing people doubt and question Me the way you do. With Raziel, be quiet and listen."

"OK, God."

We were both still for a long time. Eventually, I broke the silence by asking, "God, angels don't really talk like that to one another, do they?"

God laughed. "No."

"Good."

We sat in silence until I fell asleep.

****

When I awoke, Raziel had returned.

"Whatever you want to teach me, I'm ready to learn."

"Lie down," Raziel said. "I don't want you to fall and be hurt."

I did as I was told, lying on the floor in front of the window. Outside it was still dark.

The angel moved beside me and leaned in toward my ear. I closed my eyes, not knowing what to expect. I was a little anxious about what was to come.

Raziel put their left hand on my right arm. Their hand was cold, the nails a little too long to be comfortable for me. I shivered. I felt them put their lips just beside my right ear, almost grazing it. As they did, my entire body began to vibrate. Raziel started to speak, to whisper in that language I recognized, but did not understand, the language I describe as like Hebrew, but more guttural. It is the expression in verbal form of math, the language of God and the angels.

Raziel spoke rhythmically, chanting. I felt dizzy. Energy surged inside me. I convulsed, like a puppet moved by unseen strings. The angel continued to speak, keeping their mouth close to my ear no matter how my head moved or my spine contorted. My body flopped around, lifting and twisting into bizarre shapes.

After a few minutes, my consciousness shifted. I no longer felt frightened, but instead experienced a sense of unitive awareness with the world around me. I didn't so much know as experience the 'oneness' of God. I felt, too, what God meant when He called Himself the great 'I am'—the 'is-ness' of God. As I felt this understanding grow within myself, I began to chant with Raziel in the divine language. Still with their face to my ear, when I started to chant, Raziel's voice became louder, commanding the knowledge they imparted to enter my soul. I floated upward, still flailing and contorting.

Raziel stepped back from me, their hands making symbols near me, but moving so quickly I could not see what the gestures were. I continued to sing, declaring that the knowledge Raziel was passing to me would be used for the betterment of the world.

I fell abruptly to the floor. The room was silent except for my gasping. Raziel was at the window, gazing at the ocean.

When I got my breath back, I said, "I would like to ask a question now."

Raziel laughed. Their laugh was charming, much lighter than God's. "Now would be an appropriate interval for a question," they said.

"What did you just do to me?"

"I spoke into your soul, in the language of creation, all that is relevant for you to know. To be able to speak into the hearts of others, you must know something of God's true being. As a human, you will never fully know this. However, there is an incantation that allows you to experience the expansiveness of God's being in the limited ways your body and senses will allow.

"It is important to know God's 'one-ness,' His singularity. Prior to Judaism there was no concept among men, at least not in any organized way, of God as a singular force. That's where idolatry comes from. When humankind worshipped God as sun, rain, and fertility, they did so because that is how they experienced the world. Idols reinforced that fractured understanding of divinity. This is why God is adamant that no idols be worshipped. God is not splintered, but is manifest in all things. God is all. Literally, God is everything.

"You sometimes describe the way you see God as being a needle on a tree. You know that what you see is only a small piece or representation of the whole, but it cannot describe the whole. Let's use that analogy in a different way. Take for example the pine tree outside this window. If we equate the tree with the entire universe, then we could call the tree God. God is the manifestation of all things, as well as everything we call no-thing. If you take one needle off that tree, you cannot call that needle 'God.' It is not the whole nor is it a complete picture of what goes into the entirety of the tree. Instead of thinking of the needle as how you see God, think of the needle as yourself. You are a piece of the whole and a manifestation of divine grace. You are a manifestation of divinity.

"More than that, along with God's singularity, God is also creativity itself, not a being, but the essence of all that is creative, the consciousness of the creative spark. God called all things into being, from nothingness into form. God used language, not because it was necessary, but because in creating humankind in His image, God gave you the power of creation. God let Adam name all the plants and animals in this world, thereby giving humans responsibility for the world's stewardship. God intended mankind to be His creative, powerful custodians for this garden you call Earth. Just as God spoke the world into being and I continue that creation on Mount Horeb, so too does humankind have the power to create a radical new world through both words and deeds."

"How?" I asked.

"Do you think it is a mistake or coincidence that God asked you to write a book?"

I thought about this for a moment. "I assumed God asked me to write a book because I'm a writer."

"No. God chose a writer because words chosen with careful intention have the power to change actions. Words change the world. Words become stories. Stories arouse action. You and all human beings can call into being what you dream the world to be through your words. Your intentions and actions will follow your words."

I wished I had as much confidence in myself as God seemed to have in me, but I did not share these doubts aloud, because I believed that what Raziel had to say about the creative power of language was true. Instead, I considered Raziel's words until I began to believe them.

If Raziel was reading my thoughts, they did not let on. They continued, "The creative power of what you consider magic or sorcery is based on mastery of the divine language. There are those who seek this power, the power of names, in the Torah. There are clues there, but that is not the purpose for which Torah was given."

I repositioned myself on the floor because my feet were starting to tingle as they fell asleep. I wanted to remember everything Raziel told me. They had given me the gift of learning that had been asked of them, whispering secrets into my ear. I was shaken by the enormity of the bequest. I felt a surge of power within me. I knew suddenly that I could make the winds dance and uproot trees on a whim. I could make it rain or keep rain from coming. I could read men's minds and change their actions. With this power came a feeling of self-satisfaction and greed. My stomach lurched. I knew that my time with Raziel was coming to an end. Before I could reconsider, I said, "Raziel, please take from me the conscious knowledge of how to use the powers you have bestowed upon me. I don't trust myself to use them with wisdom or charity."

For the first time since we met, a genuine smile graced Raziel's face. "You have more wisdom than you give yourself credit for," they said. They came over to me and placed their hand on my head. Instantly, I felt a burst of heat and then a return to a more normal state of being. Gone were the thoughts of power and control. Back were my insecurities and racing fears. It was a good trade. I was made to be human.

I smiled at Raziel. "Thank you," I said before watching them disappear.

I needed to sleep. The experience I'd just had with Raziel was overwhelming. My body was heavy and tired, yet my mind was alert. My spirit soared with an energy and vitality that I had never before experienced. I understood, as fully as any human being is able, the oneness and specialness of God. I had felt it in my body. This was not the intellectual understanding I'd gotten from my studies of Judaism and consciousness, but a visceral knowledge of the soul. God is everything, as the expression goes. "God is one," I whispered quietly in Hebrew.

****

Chapter Nine

כל ישראל ערבים זה לזה

All of Israel is responsible for one another.
– Babylonian Talmud, Shevuot 39a

It was Elul, the end of September, almost the High Holy Days, and nearly a year since I made a commitment to write about the visionary experiences God had given me. I had had a difficult few weeks since I had been visited by Raziel. I was doing my best to live as I knew was expected of me, but I found it extremely challenging. For example, though I knew it was best to eat meat only occasionally and to buy local, farm-raised meat that had been humanely slaughtered, I still found myself sliding into the fast food drive-through for something quick and inexpensive. I tried to raise some of my own vegetables, but they needed too much attention, and what didn't die was quickly eaten by rabbits. When I needed new t-shirts to work in the barn, I went to the store and bought cheap products that were almost certainly made by underpaid or child laborers in the Far East. I lost my temper on the phone with customer service agents who put me on hold for interminable periods and left me on my last nerve with their inability to provide any service at all. I felt sorry for myself for not having all the goods and experiences in life I'd hoped for. In short, I felt like whatever Raziel had done to me had not taken hold. I knew how I was supposed to live, but like someone cheating on a diet, I couldn't quite keep myself on track.

God visited again while I was blowing my shofar at the end of my recitation of the Ma'ariv prayers. I had always liked the sound of the shofar and had been blessed to have been taught how to blow one. I have a beautiful horn from Yemen, and though it tastes like the underside of a horse's hoof, the sound that emanates from it is pure inspiration. As I finished my tekiah gedolah and pulled the shofar from my lips, God appeared. He was in a hurry.

"No more wasting time berating yourself for your imperfections. Come with Me."

I stood on a dirt path in Nepal. We were in the high Himalayas, but below the tree line. I had been in this part of the world once before, on a path very much like this one. As my guide and I walked down the steep, slippery slope, I wondered how in the world we would return from our destination. I was in far too poor physical condition to walk back the way we had come. We ended up hitchhiking back to my hotel. We paid a truck driver a considerable sum to take us back. I was grateful, on this evening, that God made me able to stand and walk on the mountainside with ease.

A young man with a very elderly woman on his back rushed past me. He was shabbily dressed in pants and a jacket so worn they could have provided little warmth. He had no shoes. The woman looked to be at least a hundred, but was probably closer to seventy-five or eighty. She was bundled in equally threadbare clothes, though she had a lot of them on.

198

She held tight to the man's chest, her legs wrapped around his hips, her bottom cradled in his arms. Most notable were her features. She had a dark, heavily creased face and cloudy yellow pupils in her eyes. She had cataracts and was completely blind.

Cataracts are regularly treated in the West. People all over the planet develop them with age. In North America, Europe, Australia, Japan, and other wealthy nations, the removal and replacement of the lens is a relatively common procedure. But in remote parts of Asia, Africa, and South America, cataracts mean blindness. Too few doctors are available to perform the surgery, and too few people who need it can access those doctors or afford the procedure. And so there is needless suffering in the poorer nations of the world.

I followed this pair down the mountain a short distance to a school. I knew it was a school because there was a chalkboard in the single classroom in the building. Otherwise, it was a decrepit building with mudbrick sides and a tin roof. I couldn't imagine the kind of dedication to learning it would take to pay attention to lessons in a school like that, and my heart swelled with admiration for the children who were committed enough to education to learn there.

A line of blind people sat outside the classroom, waiting with the companions who brought them. The people who came together spoke softly to one another. A sense of hopefulness pervaded the group. Inside the schoolroom, all the desks had been removed and a makeshift surgery was set up. Nothing was state of the art, but everything was adequate.

In the surgery was a middle-aged Nepali doctor and an assistant. The doctor, seeing that everything in the surgery was set up to his liking, went outside where the potential patients waited. The old woman had been set down at the end of this line by the young man. There were approximately a dozen people in the line, each of them carried or led carefully to this school. The doctor, who was now peering into each of their faces, speaking to them softly as he did, was a volunteer who was committed to returning sight to the blind in rural Nepal. Some people called him a saint or a bodhisattva, but he shrugged off those titles. All that was important to him was restoring sight to the blind wherever he could, so that they would be able to go about their lives and take care of themselves for as long as possible.

The doctor triaged the patients, deciding whom he could help and whom he could not, then prioritized them for their surgeries. When he was done, he would go back to Kathmandu. In a month, he would return to check on his patients.

God did not bring me back, but He whispered in my ear as I watched the young man carry the old woman back up the mountain after her surgery. He told me that four weeks from now, she would walk to the school under her own power, able to see her way without any problem.

****

I found myself next in a small town. God and I were standing on the main street. The town had the idyllic feel that fictional TV shows depicted of the Midwest in the 1950s, but was completely modern. I looked around.

Here was a revitalized main street of what had probably been a near-defunct or abandoned village. The buildings were old, but refurbished. They were now home to all manner of shops, shops I was familiar with and at the same time were a taste of the past. There was no super-mega-all-in-one store or a convenience store or a department store or a big box store or even a fast food restaurant. There was a hardware store and a feed store, veterinary and medical clinics, and a diner. Across the street was a produce vendor and a butcher beside yarn and tailor shops. There were Punjabi and Ethiopian restaurants and a dojo. Around the corner, I saw a hair salon, a school, a pharmacy, and on the main square, the police station and courthouse. "It's Mayberry," I said, smiling.

"You are close," God replied. "Mayberry, though a fictional place, had a lot of positive attributes, and yet the people were real in that they were flawed. Humankind thrives in places like Mayberry."

As we walked, God continued to speak. I listened, enjoying the warm late fall afternoon sunshine which filtered through the trees that lined the sidewalk. "Human beings cannot really respect one another in large cities. You do not have to know each other. You can walk past each other without saying hello. You can have shut-ins, because one is not responsible for another. You can ignore the homeless because the problem seems overwhelming. The wealthy gain a sense of entitlement. Crime becomes sinister in its anonymity. In the world's dominant cultures and nations, people become commodities based on what they produce. A person's value is based on what they earn, not who they are and what they give to the community. Yet, even those who are too ill or young to work have value.

"But in a small town, you cannot ignore your fellows. You know the homeless, the poor, and the widow. You may still choose not to care for them, but you will know them. It is harder to ignore the hardships of those around you. It is like the images of the famine victims in Ethiopia in the 1980s. At some point, those watching in the West became inured, saturated with pictures, and shut the television off. Out of sight, out of mind. You cannot do that with a homeless man who sleeps in the doorway of the library every night and over whom you have to step on your way to work."

I sat down on a park bench in the green space in front of the courthouse. There was a large tree with brilliant red leaves shading us. The air was perfumed with the scent of falling leaves and birdsong wafted through the air. I wasn't sure life got any better than this. I understood what God was saying. The American motto seemed to have become 'More. Bigger. Faster. Cheaper.' There was little regard for the consequences of that quest. Sitting on that park bench, I liked the idea of going to the butcher for fresh meat, humanely raised and slaughtered on a local farm. I liked the idea of buying a piece of furniture from a carpenter whose children went to the local school. I liked the idea of purchasing an antique piece from an old woman who ran a quiet shop and cherished every item she traded. I wanted a life in which human interactions and artisanship had meaning.

"This is what you are missing," God said. "Simple living. Fresh fruit shared with friends and a band playing on a warm midsummer night."

"I had that when I was a girl," I said. "In the small town near where I grew up, we had community like that.

"When I was fourteen, our house burned down in the night. I was lucky to get out of the fire alive and without injury. We had nothing. What I remember most was how people came to help. One neighbor loaned us a small travel

202

trailer to live in. Another brought over a camper so that we'd have some space and privacy. Others brought food, furniture, and bedding. I still have the quilt that a group of elderly women made for people in our circumstances. The members of my 4-H club knew I'd lost the clothes I wore when I showed my horse. They pitched in and gave me a gift certificate to buy a new pair of show boots and a hat. Although I gave the hat away to another 4-H member many years ago, I can't part with the boots because they're a symbol of how much people cared about me."

"That is the type of community I am talking about," God said. "Elinor, what if the same principles of community and caring were applied to all human needs? What if the only way to raise and sell produce was locally and organically? What would access to healthcare look like if doctors could simply practice to the best of their abilities and not be burdened with the concerns of litigious patients, exorbitant malpractice insurance rates, and insurance companies that do not want to pay for much of anything? What would homes look like if furniture came from artisans with whom you had a personal relationship? What if, knowing you had to live in the filth you created, you used wind or solar power to generate electricity for your homes and to power electric vehicles? What if charitable giving was a way of life, not an afterthought or a means to get a tax deduction? What if international trade was for items necessary, but unavailable locally, like some minerals, and most travel was for cultural and artistic exchange? What if price-gouging was not tolerated? What if people could practice their religions in peace, without judgment or imposing their views on others? What would the world look like then?"

"You want us to live simple, quasi-agrarian lives. No hierarchy. No lust for abundance. No intolerance of others. It sounds straightforward and impossible at the same time. I should know, God. I've been trying and failing miserably."

"It is not impossible at all," God said. "It is a matter of values and priorities, of prioritizing connection instead of commodity. You can collectively choose to live with compassion.

"The truth is simple. If you want your children to live, as a society you must change. You must live within your means in every way. This resource binge cannot continue. You see the warning signs. They are everywhere. Do you not hear the scientists talking about mass extinction? What, other than roaches, is not endangered? Bears. Whales. Sharks. Big cats. Elephants. Rhinos. Primates. Nearly every species of large animal in the world is threatened by the machinations of the global economy. You cannot continue to deny that humans too are large animals. You are not outside the ecosystems you are destroying."

The sun was beginning to set. I leaned on God, laying my head against His form like a little girl might. He made Himself more solid for me. Though it was beautiful, if you looked beyond the surface, it was easy to see that this town was as imperfect as any other. As I sat with my head on God's shoulder, I heard a man yelling at his wife. I saw a thin dog take a piece of half-rancid meat from behind the butcher shop. I saw an old man peek through drawn curtains to watch the world pass by. I knew that somewhere a woman was working as a prostitute because she needed to, and a man was hopelessly drunk. Before long, we'd need to vacate this bench, which would be a young person's bed for the night. This place was no utopia, but it was a start.

What it was, was livable. There were no large vehicles on the roads, only pedestrians, motor scooters, and golf carts. The homes and businesses all had solar panels on their roofs, some of them very cleverly disguised. A sign near the outskirts of town directed people to the wind farm. The air was sweet, and overall, even though the town was bustling as people went about their business, it was relatively quiet. I could definitely see myself living here, with a backyard garden and several large fruit trees.

Problems of racism, sexism, and other forms of bigotry and prejudice would not be erased piecemeal. Though it looked familiar in many ways, this 'Mayberry' was radical. It could not exist based on structures and systems rooted in oppression. And it was only one example of what a compassionate community might look like. I could imagine other forms of interaction that were just as compassionate, but based in a different culture. In this place, I genuinely felt that not only could we choose change, but that the other alternative was death. As imperfect as this town was, I preferred it to what we presently had and felt it was a real opportunity to improve relationships and build a future.

"Elinor," God said quietly, "people are happier when they have less. The King of Bhutan said it best when he said that it is gross national happiness, not gross national product, that is important. Work less and spend more time with your family. Buy less and buy local, artisan-made products that are quality and will last, or buy antique or repurposed items. You will never regret an extra book read to your child or a meal with friends, just as you will never lie on your deathbed and say that you wish you had written one more report at the office.

"The world is in crisis. Change is possible, but if you do not drastically transform your values and way of life now, it will soon be too late for all."

****

Back at my home, God asked me, "Do you remember the vision you had about the German book?"

I did indeed. Several months earlier, around Tisha b'Av, I had seen the cover of a book in a dream. Its title was *Von den Jüden und iren Lügen*—in English, *On Jews and Their Lies.*

In the dream, I stood in a small, one-room building with a wood panel interior. The book I'd seen was on a wooden pulpit in the front of the room. A man, who looked like a minister, opened the book, reading aloud from it to a group of perhaps two dozen laborers sitting in pews, poor peasants seeking meaning for their hardship and hope for their lives. Though the man read in German, I understood every word. His tone was angry, pointed, urging the people to action. The listeners were moved by his rhetoric, giving vocal affirmation and nodding their heads. I listened, too.

The reader claimed that Jews are under the influence of the devil and his minions. He said that synagogues are the dens of these devils, and as such synagogues and all Jewish homes should be burned to the ground. The Jews, he read, should be housed like animals in barns. He continued, demanding that the Jews be enslaved and the rabbis put to death. The words coming out of the man's mouth were so vile

I could not stay. I turned, ran from the building, and forced myself awake.

I got on my computer immediately and typed the German book title into the search engine. I learned that this horrible book had been written in 1543 by well-known Protestant Reformation leader Martin Luther. I stared at the screen. The first link sent me to a long article. How could I not have been taught that Martin Luther was an anti-Semite? His anti-Semitic writings are everywhere, easily accessible in the electronic age. Though I had never doubted my visions before, this I had difficulty believing. Hitler, I understood as pathologically murderous, but Martin Luther? How could anyone who called himself a religious reformer hate a whole people as mightily as this?

Recalling all of this, I nodded slowly at God. "Yes, I remember it well," I said cautiously, not sure where God was taking the conversation.

"Why did you run away, wake yourself from the dream?"

"Because I had seen and heard enough," I said emphatically. "Who wants to stand by and hear their family, their people, referred to as devils, as being worthy only of slave labor or death? I have no interest in that kind of vitriol."

"Excellent," God said. "I want this to be very clear to you, Elinor, because it is extremely important and undergirds all of My interaction with humankind and creation." God paused. "I created mankind to be responsible for one another. First, you co-create the world with Me through language, intention, and action. Second, you are to provide for one another that which you hope and pray I will provide to you."

All people are responsible for each other. The way forward could be as simple as that.

****

Chapter Ten

נר ה׳ נשמת אדם חפש כל־חדרי־בטן

The spirit of man is the lamp of God, revealing all his inner parts.

– Proverbs 20:27

The small pumpkin patch I planted just beyond the roses was producing abundantly. I'd put in several varieties, all of which were good for eating. There were perhaps three dozen orange spheres of various sizes waiting to be plucked from the plants. To behold it was a backyard gardener's delight. I had pulled out four large apple boxes in which to harvest my bounty, but it wasn't enough. I unloaded the first four boxes into the back seat of the car, then went back to the garden for the next load.

I was standing in the cool soil, picking ripe pumpkins from the vines, when I felt God's presence behind me. I spoke without turning. "You have to wait until I'm done here. I am taking most of these pumpkins to the synagogue. We'll make pies and take them to the food bank to be given away for Thanksgiving." I was deeply committed to this project. In our current political state, Jews making pies for the poor was an act of civic defiance.

God said nothing. When I was finished picking the pumpkins, I turned toward where He waited. I was smiling broadly.

"You seem happy," God said.

"I am," I replied. "Things are different with me since we last spoke."

"I would like you to speak about that."

"OK, but let me take these pumpkins to the car first."

I stepped carefully out of the pumpkin patch and walked easily along the pea-gravel path to the garage, making four trips with my crates full of pumpkins. Once inside, I heaved four crates of pumpkins into the back of my car. It was completely filled by my harvest. I had far too much for a single person, even with preserving for the winter. The excess I'd pass on. I smiled, looking forward to cooking the three pumpkins I'd kept for myself, and making one into a couple of delicious, fresh pies.

When I was through, I went into the house, got myself a glass of water, and made my way into the living room. I put my glass on a coaster without taking a drink. God was on the hearth. I sat down on the couch facing Him, curling my feet up under me. "I'm glad You're here," I said.

I felt God smile. "So, talk to Me."

I thought about all the things I wanted to say to God, tried to get the ideas organized in my head. I had so much to share that I was bursting, and yet words failed me. Nothing I thought about saying felt at all adequate to describe my inner transformation. God waited patiently. Eventually I said, "The gift and challenge You set before me is magnificent. The only way to describe this new understanding is to say that I feel a sense of purpose in following the path You've laid before me.

I understand the calling of the visionary. She is on Earth to warn and teach, nothing more. What comes after is not my responsibility. I feel a weight lifted from my shoulders, a weight that I put there that did not ever need to be.

"But You've got a different role. You soothe our souls. You support my spirit. You love me when I have no one else."

God moved from the hearth to the couch and embraced me. I cried only for a few moments. When I was done, God wiped the tears from my face. "You are very brave," He said. I smiled. "Are you ready for the last part of this journey, the final vision that you are to share in the book?" God asked.

"Yes," I said. I closed my eyes and lay back on the couch, waiting for the vision God would give me.

****

I opened my eyes to find myself exactly where God had left me, on the couch in my living room. I sat up and looked around. I was alone. Standing, I went to the front window to look outside. Everything looked the same, but somehow was not. I went out. Nothing had changed. The garage door was still open and the pumpkins sat, as a triumph of my gardening efforts, in the car.

I went back inside to my bedroom and sat down on my bed, my back against the headboard. I had a nagging feeling that something wasn't right, but I had no idea what it was. I turned on both the computer and the television. The television started up first. The last show I'd watched was on one of the major networks. Regular programming had been suspended. On the screen was a banner indicating that momentarily the network would offer a special report. I turned up the volume and leaned back against the pillows to wait for the news.

After a minute, the newscaster came on. Regular programming was interrupted to give viewers an update on the pandemic sweeping the nation. Researchers had not identified the virus. Symptoms suggested a flu, but the spread of the disease was faster than any known flu virus. From first symptoms to death, patients were living only three days. Nearly ninety percent of those infected died. The disease was moving so swiftly that there was no stopping it. Worse still, the contagion was airborne. Everyone was being advised not to go out for any reason. All services had been closed. There was no postal delivery, no school. All government offices had been shut, which was causing mayhem as people desperately tried to find out what would happen to their checks, from public assistance to Social Security. The government asked all stores to close, even grocery stores, though some of those had remained open to fill prescriptions and sell food until stock ran out. Private clinics closed, leaving public hospitals overrun with patients. Nearly all houses of worship closed their doors as a health precaution for congregants. Unlike in other countries, where lockdowns were required and enforced, in the U.S., staying home was more of a suggestion than a requirement. Those who believed the pandemic was a hoax refused to be told what to do or how to live.

I changed the channel. On every station were either reports of the global devastation that this virus had produced or televised prayer services. In defiance of the closures, hundreds of thousands of people in states nationwide were joining together in tent revivals, and at the same time spreading the disease. The few police who turned up to work

212

desperately tried to get the groups to disband. Doctors who had worked at the now defunct Centers for Disease Control and Prevention publicly issued warnings that disease transmission was greatest among large groups of people. Even on the televised broadcasts, as obviously ill choir members sang their praise to God, members of the congregation dropped from disease. Reporters used drones to capture images of what became of the sick. They were carried outside and laid under makeshift medical tents, where the faithful tried to heal them with the laying on of hands. The juxtaposition of prayer and death was horrifying.

I changed the channel again. Reporters in hazmat suits showed videos of widespread looting and panic in all major urban areas. In suburban and rural areas, such as where I lived, armed militias were patrolling the streets, maintaining order through violence and intimidation. In Texas, the well-armed citizenry had developed a shoot-on-sight policy for anyone unknown doing anything that seemed even mildly suspicious. In one report, I saw the body of a man a militia gunman claimed to have executed for knocking on the door of a house. It turned out that the dead man had been going to his brother's house so they could lockdown together. The gunman remained proud of his kill nonetheless. I turned off the television.

I left the bedroom and went to the kitchen. I opened the refrigerator, where I kept enough fresh food on hand to last me at least a week. I checked the pantry, which was also well-stocked with canned and dry goods. I surveyed what I had: canned and dried fruit, vegetables, soups, pasta, rice, beans, and, most important, gallons upon gallons of bottled water. In the freezer in the garage, I had meat, fruit, and vegetables.

213

Assuming the power stayed on, I had enough fresh and frozen food for at least two months.

I went to the garage and closed the door. I had taught camping skills for the Girl Scouts for more than a decade. Part of the reason I moved out of town was exactly because a situation like this could arise. The first thing to do was to gather the necessary supplies. If the situation continued to deteriorate, as I suspected that it would, chaos would rule the cities. If I needed anything at all, it had to be gathered now. The car had a full tank of gas. I also had two five-gallon gas containers filled with fuel for an emergency. Fuel would likely be the most difficult item to get if I needed to leave. With all people advised to stay home, gas stations might not be open or might run out of fuel. The pumps also would not work if the power was out. I had enough gas to get me to my uncle's house or to my friends further out in the country. Still, to be on the safe side, I moved the gas canisters into a footlocker and locked it. Better that they not be visible if someone broke into the garage.

Then I stopped myself. I had made a decision to help my fellows. I looked around at all the goods I had stored in the garage. In addition to what I had in the house, out here I had enough water for a single person for weeks, not taking into account the water in the hot water heater. I had a propane stove and fuel canisters that would last at least a month. There was a water purification kit and a month's worth of freeze-dried food. I had eight weeks of food on hand for the cats and one hundred pounds of dry dog food for the neighbors. I had tools, including hatchets and a chainsaw, in the event that firewood was needed. I also had seeds stored to plant on the golf course if it seemed that we would at any point need to turn that land into farmland. I was prepared to be a resource for my community.

Going back into the house, I filled every lidded container I could find with water and put them on the kitchen counters. I filled the bathtubs and two guest sinks to use for washing. I closed the blinds in every room to keep the house insulated and made a quick inventory of sheets, blankets, and towels. I had my first aid kit, including medical-grade masks, antibiotics, and an array of other medicines. I decided that I would take two one-gallon bottles of water and a package of bleach wipes to each of my closest neighbors, leaving them on their doorstep, so as to make no contact. I would be a resource to those in need. Beyond that, there was nothing more to do but wait and see what transpired.

I went back and sat on the couch, closing my eyes briefly. When I opened them again, God was sitting beside me. I was confused. "Was that real?" I asked.

"Let us call it a trial run," God said.

I let out a great sigh. "This is terrifying," I said to God.

"Not as terrifying as what is likely to come."

****

Weeks passed. Eventually, God and I returned to the log on the lip of the meadow at which we had so often met. It was Hanukah, and I had stuffed myself with latkes from our synagogue's latkes-making party. We held the event in our social hall in defiance of those who said we had no right to celebrate our holy days, no right even to exist. We turned off all the lights and put our menorahs in the front window for all to see. Members of other faith groups joined in our celebration. I was tired, content, and deeply proud of my community.

As God and I sat in silence, each of us left to our own thoughts, I was overwhelmed with a sense of love. Not only did I love God, but I felt profoundly the depth of God's love for humankind and all creation.

I turned to look at God sitting beside me. He was there, as always, as a mist. His patience was beyond measure. We tried Him; I tried Him. I thought back to the beginning of this journey, when I'd attempted to wriggle from His grasp by refusing for so long to do as I was asked. I had been afraid, afraid of how others might judge me. Now, I didn't care. Having experienced God's love for us and the personal healing I'd had as a result of my interactions with Him, I could do nothing but devote myself to Him.

"You love us a great deal," I said to God, breaking the silence.

"Yes, I do."

"You love us so much it's often too much for me," I said.

"Do you recall the moments when I come to you and you writhe on the floor in ecstasy, twist and scream such that someone watching you might think you're having some sort of fit?"

"How can I forget?"

God smiled. "That is My love for humankind coming through. That is My love for you. Your body was not made to handle it, but still, I cannot help but express My love."

"At Yom Kippur, the rabbi always quotes *Proverbs*, saying that a man's soul is the light of God."

"That is true. The divine spark that is your soul, that grows or diminishes through your actions in life, is the light that illuminates the world. Your soul, your divinity, the piece of you that is most recognizable as Me, grows in intensity when you act with compassion and charity, in service to Me through service to others. The brightness of your light shines not only outwardly as a beacon, but inwardly, too. It brings healing to the dark corners of self that are tucked away out of reach to everyone but Me. When these dark places experience the light and are healed, there is no more darkness within and your light shines in the world even brighter.

"Humans are the stewards of life on this planet. I have given the world to you as your home. You are here to act as My agents. You are conservators and guardians of the Earth, protectors of its resources not for yourselves but for the beings here now and for generations to come. You are the defenders of those who are powerless before you, not only the poor and wretched and hurt, but all the animals, plants, and seas."

God sighed. "The Earth will be whatever you will it to be. I will not force anything upon you. That would be intruding too much. I am suggesting, however, that you consider remaking society into something that will make all humans happier; other beings safer; that will bring you closer to Me and one another; and that will honor the planet and resources you are here to guard and develop. I am suggesting that you look at everything: how you eat; the energy sources you use; the ways you interact with one another; your personal value and the overvaluing of money and economics; the importance you place on the items you own; how you help the suffering; and the time you spend developing your spirits. Are you willing to live within your means so that those who come after you will have an opportunity to live at all? Change in ways that create community and foster respect. Or do not change, if this is the best life and future you can see for yourselves and coming generations. You are at the tipping point of disaster or transformation. Your choice. Embrace your gluttony and revel in your excess or transform your communities. But do something. This blind spin into oblivion is a degradation of your souls."

"We are doomed by our choices."

"Likely," God replied.

"*The Book of Life* is sealed," I whispered.

"*The Book of Life* is written in pencil, Elinor, and you each hold the piece of lead that inscribes your collective destiny."

****

Afterword

שמע עצה וקבל מוסר למען תחכם באחריתך

Listen to counsel and receive advice that you may be wise in the end.

– Proverbs 19:20

This is the end of the story I was asked to tell. It is up to you to decide what to do with it. You decide the veracity of this prophecy. Is it a work of fiction that entertains and may or may not have applications to your everyday experience in the world, or is it a thinly veiled message of truth? Am I a charlatan, a huckster, a snake-oil vendor, a false prophet who has an ulterior motive, who wants you to follow me for my gain, or is this a genuine wake-up call sent by God, using an imperfect messenger, to shake you from your complacency and call you to action?

I am afraid. I fear that I have not done my job well enough and that you will continue as you always have, going to yoga, sometimes eating a vegan meal, and recycling your bottles and cans, thinking that you have done your part and made your contribution to the world. Those actions are insufficient.

We are under threat. Climate change is real. Our democratic institutions have been undermined. We marginalize and abuse people who are in some way different from 'us.' We value money over life. We are on the brink of disaster.

Resist. Defy the powers that be and take action. Get off the grid if you can. Put solar panels on your roof or install a windmill if you need power to your barn. Buy an electric car. Better yet, get bicycles for the whole family. Plant a garden. Plant trees, fruit trees when possible. Learn a skill—knitting, canning, beekeeping. Eat a lot less meat. Buy organic products. Vote, not for a party, but for candidates who are willing to debate issues, compromise, and come up with solutions that benefit the community, not a specific subset of constituents or industries. Demand real action on climate change at the local, state, national, and international levels. Protest! Learn to discern between genuine news reporting, propaganda, and 'fake news.' The latter are intended to distract. Support the library and the food bank and, above all, prepare your children for the worst.

I am not God. I do not believe in you or your capacity to change. I find human beings to be selfish and self-serving. But I also know that change is possible. I have turned my life around, become someone I never envisioned I would be. This isn't the life that I imagined for myself, but it is a good life. Is it possible that the kind of personal transformation I have experienced is not one in a million, but something that can happen at the level of society? Can millions, billions of us make the same kind of complete life change? Can we shift our focus to compassion and service, leaving selfishness and greed behind?

Believe that it can happen and take action, if not for you, for your children. There is no time left for talk. The period for debate has passed. If you want your children to have any hope of surviving, of seeing the twenty-second century, you must take radical action now.

I don't have a horse in this race. I am middle-aged and childless. The complete breakdown of the climate should begin around 2050. While I probably will not be dead, I will already be old. It doesn't matter what becomes of me. But your children will be in the prime of their lives. If you care about them, change your life. Today.

You will only get one warning from me. This is it. Believe it.

****

About the Author

Ahuva Batya (Constance) Scharff, PhD is an internationally recognized speaker and award-winning author. She speaks and writes on the topics of addiction and trauma recovery, the psychological impacts of climate change, women's leadership, and decolonizing mental health. She is the founder of the Institute for Complementary and Indigenous Mental Health Research and a passionate advocate for access to mental healthcare and radical social transformation to lessen the impacts of climate change. Her nonfiction books center around using complementary mental health practices to improve treatment outcomes. Her poetry and fiction highlight spiritual experience and connection to the divine. *The Path to God's Promise* is her first novel.

Printed in the USA
CPSIA information can be obtained
at www.ICGtesting.com
LVHW012124061023
760367LV00004B/257